A Deadly Game . . .

Jake turned on the television, grabbed a Pepsi, and opened the pizza. There was an envelope fastened to the inside top of the box. He felt his head start hammering as he saw the lettering on the envelope.

E2C1F2G1   CANCELLED

He was familiar enough with the code to know it spelled his name. His hand was shaking as he removed the envelope from the lid. It was a single piece of paper. It read:

D1B3G2G2G1A3D2B2D1C3C1F3F1

He grabbed a pencil, and a minute later he'd translated. The message simply said BULLETIN BOARD.

He raced to his room and switched on the computer. Jake entered his personal code. As the screen filled with the code Jake's heart sank. He reached for the disk labeled CODEBREAKER. He read his translation of the message:

Your father sent you this dinner. We have him here in Cairns. If you mention any of this to any person—any person at all—you will never see your father alive again. If you want to save his life, behave normally. Be inside the international terminal by the Cent... ...
8:00 A.M. tomor...
to the letter or e...
nication. Our p...

D1430467

CODE
of
DECEPTION

Ted Ottley

BANTAM BOOKS
NEW YORK • TORONTO • LONDON • SYDNEY • AUCKLAND

for the Spaniels

RL 7.0, age 012 and up

CODE OF DECEPTION

A Bantam Book / published by arrangement with the author
June 1996

The Starfire logo is a registered trademark of Bantam Books, a
division of Bantam Doubleday Dell Publishing Group, Inc.
Registered in U.S. Patent and Trademark Office and elsewhere.

ISBN 0-553-56754-3

Published simultaneously in the United States and Canada

Bantam Books are published by Bantam Books, a division of Bantam
Doubleday Dell Publishing Group, Inc. Its trademark, consisting of the
words "Bantam Books" and the portrayal of a rooster, is Registered in
U.S. Patent and Trademark Office and in other countries. Marca
Registrada. Bantam Books, 1540 Broadway, New York, New York
10036.

PRINTED IN THE UNITED STATES OF AMERICA

OPM 0 9 8 7 6 5 4 3 2 1

CODE
of
DECEPTION

prologue

chapter one

four months later

Lila Spooner always walked her dog, Heidi, by the same route at the same time every day. You could set your watch by it. She turned the corner of Garden Road at precisely 4:28 P.M. By 5:30 she stopped —or rather her dachshund, Heidi, did—opposite Claremont Boys' High School. At 5:35 P.M. Ted Johnson, the owner of the white bungalow, cursed Lila Spooner as he cleaned up after Heidi's latest deposit. Lila did not believe in cleaning up after her pet; in fact, Lila cared for very little but snooping and gossip. This Friday, she hit the jackpot—she was at the right place at the perfect time.

Heidi's ears jerked up just before Lila heard the fire engine's sirens. As she turned the corner she saw the smoke coming from the school. "Quickly, Heidi, quickly," she snapped. But Heidi stiffened her stubby legs in classic canine braking stance. Lila turned with a scolding. "Oh, really, Heidi, not *now*!"

1

That's when she saw something that would bother her for days to come.

Across the street, a dark-haired young man with a beige briefcase sprinted away from the school. Lila watched him head toward an old beat-up yellow Datsun, but at that moment the fire engine screamed to a stop opposite and blocked her view. By the time she dragged Heidi to where she could see the yellow car, it had disappeared.

Heidi began whimpering as she attempted to tow Lila away from the worsening smell of smoke. Lila tugged the dog closer to the action. She liked details when she told a story. And this one was developing very nicely indeed.

A craggy-looking man with coveralls on fire staggered from the school toward the fire engine. Screaming, he attempted to beat out the flames rapidly enveloping him. One of the firefighters raced toward him with a fireproof blanket. She threw it over the man, pushed him to the ground, and quelled the blaze. The others finished hooking up two fire hoses and directed water at the base of the flames. The hissing of steam was immediately accompanied by the whine of an ambulance.

The firefighter with the blanket yelled to the ambulance: "Over here! Got a burn victim—looks like he's in shock!" Grabbing a medical bag and respirator, the ambulance men raced over and rapidly assessed the situation. One of them cut the blackened sleeve off the patient's coveralls and frowned at the charred flesh. He selected a wet bandage from his kit and eased it onto the charred skin. The injured man groaned as the other paramedic put the oxygen mask in place: "You're gonna be okay, sir—just take some nice deep breaths for me."

By now Lila and Heidi were almost a yard from the paramedics. "I saw the whole thing—I was here all the t—"

"Lady, will you stand back while we concentrate on the patient? And get that dog outta here."

"I'm just trying to be helpful!"

"Then talk to the police when they get here. That's their department," he said, dismissing her.

Indignant, Lila started to say, "Well, I never," but something in the ambulance driver's face told her the conversation was over. Recovering her dignity, she addressed the dachshund instead. "Come, Heidi, our help doesn't seem to be appreciated here."

The pair waddled away from the immediate vicinity and prepared to cross the street. Lila was so engrossed in the afternoon's events, she stepped off the curb and into the path of a speeding bicycle.

"Look out!" Jake yelled as he slammed on the hand brakes as hard as he could. The BMX skidded to a stop so suddenly that Jake hit the pavement hard. Picking himself up, he said, "Look before you cross the road, you stupid old b—"

He stopped himself in midsentence. Oh no. It was her. What a bummer.

"Jake Carson!" exploded Lila, squinting up at his perfect pale blue eyes. "I'm sure your grandmother will be most upset to hear how you speak to her friends."

"Well, you're supposed to look before you cross the street," Jake said reasonably.

"I did," she lied. "You were riding far too fast. Far too fast indeed. Anyway, this is not a racetrack —it's a public street. And besides, I was concentrating. I have important things to report to the police."

"Well, here's your chance, Mrs. Spooner—there's the squad car," Jake said. He indicated the slowing car. Inside were two men—one an older, hard-looking man and the other a very young Asian man.

Lila hurried over to the car. Before the door could open she was volunteering information.

"I saw everything. I was here before the fire engines. Before the ambulance. And I also saw—"

"Talk to the lady for me, will you, Lee," said the police chief to the young officer driving him.

"Sure thing, Chief!"

"I would rather speak to the person in charge," Lila told the chief.

Chief Pink sighed. "Well, Mrs. Spooner, the officer here is in charge of talking to any witnesses. He'll be happy to take your statement."

The young cop shot his eyes heavenward and took out his notepad as his superior headed for the ambulance. The paramedics had just placed the burn victim on the stretcher.

"Still just one?" asked the chief. The radio opera-

4

tor had apprised him of the situation. The ambulance man nodded. "The new janitor—a Mr. Redlum. Thank God school was out for the weekend. Otherwise . . ."

"Too right," agreed the chief. "Can I talk to your patient?"

"Well, he's a little hazy, but he'll be okay. We just want to get a different dressing before this dries out. But a couple of minutes won't hurt."

"Well, now," the chief addressed the man on the stretcher. "This is no way to welcome a new man, is it?" A big, comfortable man of sixty-two, Chief Pink had an affable nature that seemed strangely at odds with his cold gray eyes.

The janitor's attempted smile became a wince, and his eyes turned to the dressing on his arm.

"Must hurt like hell," said the chief. "Anyway, they tell me you'll be back on the job in no time. Can't keep guys from our generation down, can they now. Tell me, how do you think this thing started?"

"Smelled smoke and . . . went to . . . supply room. Had to put it out. . . . The chemicals there are . . . uh . . ."

"I understand. You did a brave thing, Mr. Redlum. It would have been easier—and a lot safer—to run." Leaning slightly farther into the ambulance, he continued: "But have you any idea what could have caused the fire?"

"Dunno. Boys maybe. Sneak in sometimes . . . for a smoke I guess. And . . ."

"Well, we'll check it out." Then, to the ambulance men: "Okay, boys, won't keep you any longer —you can take him over to emergency."

"Please . . . no hospital . . . please . . . have to go back . . . my things, the . . ."

"Now, Mr. Redlum," soothed the chief, "everything here is perfectly safe. Nobody enters this area, and nobody removes a thing until we've cleared it." He gave him a reassuring pat on the shoulder.

"But I . . ." As the pain intensified, the janitor sighed. Observing his distress, the ambulance man cracked a painkilling ampoule under the janitor's nose, waited until he relaxed, then closed the door. As the ambulance headed for the inner-city hospital, the siren began its wailing.

"I got here as soon as I could, Max," the principal said, approaching the chief. "Thought maybe I could help."

"Well, there's really nothing much you can do, Martin." The chief turned to Lee. "You get a statement from that old witch?"

"Yeah, Chief. Took her forever to tell me (a) there was a fire, and (b) the new janitor came out with his clothing on fire. She's really something."

"What she *is* is a lot of trouble. When she's not gossiping she's complaining. Waste of everyone's time," the chief said with annoyance.

"What she's doing now is raising hell with some poor kid for riding his bike the wrong way," Lee observed, looking toward Lila and Jake.

The principal chuckled. "That's young Jake Carson—our computer wiz. We haven't officially met,

6

Officer. I'm the principal, Martin Oliver." The men shook hands.

Chief Max Pink preempted any further socializing. "Well, we better take a look around while it's still light—who knows, we might even get home in time for dinner."

They walked into the school through the computer lab and into the small room where various cleaning and painting supplies were kept. The air was still acrid. Heat and moisture had combined to make the humidity unbearable.

The chief wiped beads of sweat from his forehead. "Phew! Big cleanup needed here," he said. "Well, whatever caused it probably went right up in smoke. Think we better just write this off as an accident, probably caused by kids getting in here and playing with matches, or maybe the older boys having a cigarette."

"But, Chief, shouldn't we contact the arson boys? Could have been a deliberate attempt to—"

"Now, Officer," the chief said, "it's obviously a simple accidental fire. If that suits the principal here, I don't think it merits a big fuss being made. Martin? What do you think?"

The principal answered quickly—too quickly, it seemed. "I agree. I'll give the students a good firm lecture at assembly on Monday." Turning to the young officer, he added, "Boys are always doing something they shouldn't. Probably just decided to sneak in here and have a cigarette—another case of boys being boys, you might say. In any case, no great harm's been done."

7

"Absolutely," said the chief. "Now, let's get some fresh air. Lee, I'll take the car and radio for someone to give you a hand locking up. Now let's get out of this steam bath." He gestured for the men to follow him.

■ *Trouble with being young,* thought Lee, *nobody pays any attention to you!* Then, realizing the principal hadn't left the supply room, he called toward the door: "Mr. Oliver, you okay in there?"

"Just retying a shoelace that came undone." Martin Oliver was making sure the policemen were out of sight. Satisfied, he lifted his foot to reveal the half-filled hypodermic he had seen and concealed when they first entered the room. Carefully, he picked up the needle and squirted its amber contents into the charred floor, wrapped the hypodermic in his handkerchief, placed it in his jacket pocket, and left the blackened room. As he caught up with the officer, he handed him a set of keys. "You'll need these to lock up. Right now, I better get over to the hospital to see how our new janitor's getting along."

The principal got into his ancient white Jaguar and drove off. As Lee escorted the chief toward the squad car, Lila planted herself squarely in their path. "Chief Pink! Nobody around here seems to be the least bit interested in my information about this fire."

"The officer took your statement, Mrs. Spooner, and we've done a thorough investigation. It was a

8

simple, accidental blaze. The excitement's over and the case . . . is . . . closed."

"But what about the dark young man?" Lila demanded.

The chief looked at Lee.

"Mrs. Spooner thinks she saw someone running away from the fire," Lee explained. "A young guy with dark hair, had a briefcase of some sort."

"This, uh, suspect of yours. Did you actually see him coming out of the school?" the chief asked her.

"Well, not exactly, but he was coming from that direction—and he got into a yellow car. I think."

"You think," said the chief with exaggerated patience. "And you say he came from the *direction* of the school? Not much to go on." He smiled patronizingly at Lila. "Sometimes we read far too much into simple cases." He eased his substantial bulk into the squad car. "I think the best thing to do now is for all of us to go home and have a nice quiet dinner." He slammed the door, started the engine, and added, "Anyhow, that stupid little hound of yours looks like it's starving to death." As Lila turned crimson with anger, the chief drove off chuckling to himself. Lila had done nothing but spread malicious rumors about everybody—including his wife—since they'd first heard of her. It wasn't big revenge, but it was still sweet.

Lila turned to see Jake and the officer desperately trying to suppress their laughter. "Quickly, Heidi." She turned on her squat heel and dragged the bewildered dachshund away.

Somehow, Jake and the young Korean-Australian officer managed to control themselves until Lila turned the corner and disappeared. Only then did they submit to an uncontrolled laughter that brought tears to their eyes. When the moment passed, they looked at each other almost sheepishly and started laughing all over again. This time it was quieter, and finally it was over.

"Oh boy. I'm supposed to be more serious," Lee confessed.

"Well, I'm going to be in trouble when she tells my grandmother I was rude to her."

"I'll bet. Anyhow, I'm Officer—ah, never mind the formalities, I'm Lee."

"I know. I teach your kid brother swimming. I'm Jake Carson," replied the fifteen-year-old as they shook hands.

"You're the computer wiz he keeps telling us about."

Jake looked embarrassed. And a bit awkward. Just six years older, Lee could still remember what it was like to be fifteen. This kid Jake sure had everything going for him. Another year and he'd be begging the girls to leave him alone. "Tell me, Jake: What brought you here? I thought everyone got as far from this school as they could on a Friday afternoon."

Jake laughed. "Usually. But I left my computer disks and came back to get them. I'm trying to program a game about swimming."

"Maybe you're lucky you weren't here. Janitor got a nasty burn on his arm putting out the fire."

"You mean Old Redders?"

"*Who?*"

"The new janitor—don't know his real name. Kids just call him Old Redders. He doesn't mind. He's a good guy." Suddenly concerned, Jake asked, "Is he going to be okay?"

"I guess he'll be sore for a while." Then: "Well, better lock up. The other car ought to be here any minute."

"Hey, have you got the key to the computer lab?" Jake asked eagerly.

"Imagine so. The principal gave me his set."

"Do you think you could get me my disks? There's just two of them. Beside the keyboard on workstation three."

"I don't know." The officer frowned. "Nothing's supposed to leave the building."

"Oh no." Jake was disappointed. "I wanted to work on my program for the weekend. You sure they meant our personal disks as well?"

"Well, look. If you were to go in there after I'd unlocked the room . . . and I didn't know . . ." Lee winked. He turned his back on Jake and walked first to the computer lab, then down the main hallway and out of sight.

Jake didn't wait for him to reconsider. He headed straight for the computer lab and the disks on workstation three. *That's weird,* he thought, *computer's still on. I'm sure I powered off. Oh well . . .*

He followed standard shutdown procedure. The Mac buzzed as it automatically ejected a disk. Puzzled, Jake thought, *Well, I know I didn't have three disks so wh*—

His thought was interrupted by the sound of heavy footsteps in the corridor. And a gruff voice. "Lee, you there?" The footsteps came nearer.

It was the other cop. Jake hid all three disks in his pocket.

From farther away he heard Lee's voice echoing down the hallway: "I'm over here." Jake froze as the other cop's footsteps stopped, then receded. When he heard distant conversation, he switched off the Power Mac and cautiously peered around the doorway. The coast was clear. Silently, he crept down the hall to the main door, went outside, mounted his bike, and furiously pedaled for home. But as he rode, he couldn't stop wondering why the computer had been running, and what the third disk was all about.

chapter two

Martin Oliver drove his Jag into the parking lot outside the emergency room. Looking for a parking space, he wondered how many times he'd raced an injured student to this hospital. Every year seemed to bring a broken arm, a twisted ankle, or—worst of all—a bleeding wound. Now he kept a plastic sheet in the trunk in case something threatened to mar the restored morocco leather upholstery. He was grateful the state ambulance service had provided the transport for Old Redders.

Old Redders indeed! The employment application showed that the janitor was quite elderly. Turning into an empty space, Oliver frowned. He hoped there'd be no unpleasant lawsuit. More to the point, he hoped the janitor wouldn't quit because of the injury. Old Redders was a real find—for once the employment agency had sent someone you could rely on.

He set the car alarm with his remote control and headed for the emergency room. As he crossed the road from the parking lot to the main entrance, a yellow car screeched past, nearly grazing him. Oliver pointed at the car and almost shouted, "I'll see you in my office." But before he could find a more suitable reprimand the car and its dark-haired young driver had sped away.

■ The streetlights came on as Jake parked the BMX beside the verandah and ran up three steps to the front door. The old Subaru was parked in the drive, and the kitchen light at the end of the hallway glowed through the headlights.

"Hi Dad, I'm home!"

"Just fixing myself a drink." Jim Carson grinned as he finished pouring himself a triple. Tanned and fit, he was a kind-looking man—always glad when he and his son were together. "You know, those baseball hats were designed to keep the sun off your face—so why does everyone wear them backwards?"

"To prevent skin cancer on the back of the neck, I guess," Jake bantered. "Is there any Pepsi?"

"Just put six in the fridge. How was your day?"

"We had a fire at the school," Jake said as he popped a can of his favorite soft drink.

"Bad?" His dad walked through to the living room and his favorite leather chair.

"Well, Old Redders—he's the janitor—got a burn and went to hospital. Then the cops came and Egghead Oliver was—"

"You can call him the principal, Jake."

"Yeah, well, they all checked the place out and

figured it was just an accident. Maybe some kids smoking or something."

"Not you, I hope," his father murmured as he sipped his scotch.

"I was teaching swimming—I just went back for my disks. By then it was over. But guess who was there? Old Lila Spooner. She reckoned I nearly ran over her, but she walked right onto the road without looking. Came off my bike, I had to brake so hard."

"Hope your bike's not hurt," his father said dryly. A kind of friend of his mother's, Lila had irritated Jim since he was a boy. The legend continued—here she was annoying his son.

"Bike's okay, but look." He indicated a small rip in his new 501s. "I oughta sue her for a new pair."

"Well, your grandma can mend them when she comes tomorrow."

"Oh, great." They both rolled their eyes. Saturdays were heaven and hell. Heaven because Grandma Carson could outcook anyone; hell because she tried to impose order on her son and grandson. Worse still, she forced Jake to listen to her version of the family history over and over again. Although they were glad to see her arrive, neither Jim nor Jake was saddened when she left.

Jim topped off his scotch. "Remember to clean your room before you turn in tonight."

"Awww—I got homework and stuff to do on my PC," Jake protested weakly.

"It's up to you." They both knew the pending

15

arrival of Jake's grandmother Joyce was ample reason to put things in order. It was a lot easier than having her help.

"Yeah, yeah. I will before I go to bed."

"Just don't fall asleep at the computer again. Now, what about dinner?"

Friday night was Jake's night to choose the food. Ever since his mother had left five years ago, Jake and his dad had officially proclaimed Friday junk food night. They usually phoned for two enormous pizzas with a salad. While they waited for the food to be delivered, they played the classic video game Doomkritters. Tonight was no exception. Jake phoned in the order. Jim put the silver joysticks on the coffee table. As soon as Jake finished on the phone they started in on Doomkritters—the game that held special significance for the entire Carson family.

■ Outside, a yellow car cruised by the house for the third time.

■ At the hospital Martin Oliver was becoming impatient. He'd been waiting over half an hour to speak with the intern who'd attended Old Redders. Just as he was about to ask the indifferent receptionist how long he had to wait, the flexible plastic door parted to reveal an orderly wheeling the janitor toward the exit. Old Redders was protesting: "I am quite able to walk—it's only my arm that's been hurt."

"I understand, sir. But it's hospital policy to

16

bring you to the exit in a wheelchair. Now, if you want a taxi, just pick up the yellow phone over there. It's a direct line to the cab com—"

"That won't be necessary," an authoritative voice interrupted. The orderly and janitor turned. It was the principal speaking. "I'll see Mr. Redlum is taken care of now."

Getting out of the wheelchair, Old Redders exclaimed, "Why, thank you, sir, but I can get a bus home from here. I'm feeling fine."

"Nonsense. Won't take a minute to drive you home. Car's just over here." As they got to the car the principal said, "Hope you don't mind, I'll just put a protective sheet over the leather upholstery. I'm in the next *concours d'élégance* and—"

"I quite understand, Mr. Oliver. These clothes are full of soot and smoke." He helped arrange the plastic sheet over the passenger seat. "This is very kind of you," he said, fastening the seat belt with his good arm.

As they drove, Oliver asked him about the fire, praised him for his quick action in containing the blaze, and casually brought up the topic on his mind.

"Did you see anything . . . uh . . . strange in the supply room. Like lit cigarettes or anything, you know, unusual?"

"No, there was too much smoke to see anything very clearly."

"I see. Well, did you . . . uh . . . *smell* anything strange? Like if one of the boys had lit a joint . . ."

17

"I don't think I know how that kind of thing would smell, Mr. Oliver."

"No," Oliver said gently, "but when you've been at the school longer, I'm sure you'll come across it. A sweetish smell, like herbs burning perhaps?"

"Oh, there were strange smells all right, but not like that. See, that room's full of paints and solvents and wax, and the smoke smelled like—well, burning oil. Shouldn't speak ill of the dead, I know, but the previous janitor left turpentine rags and other things lying around that he shouldn't have."

Oliver thought the man sounded suddenly tired. "This has been a terrible experience for you," he said. "Take some time off to feel better and when you come back I think we can see that you get something extra in your pay. Something substantial."

"That'd be wonderful—the money part. But I don't need time off—there are things I have to tidy up soon as I can. Anyway, don't you worry about me. The doc said I'd be just fine."

As they stopped outside Old Redders's block of apartments, the principal wondered what the janitor meant by the "other things" he claimed his predecessor shouldn't have left lying around. The question was best left unasked.

The yellow car following them braked, executed a perfect U-turn, and silently drove away.

■ The metallic crocodile snapped its metal jaws around the body and dragged it underwater.

"Oh no!" Jake's father cried in mock despair. "This time he got me first try."

The final logo came up on the screen. "You drown, Jim, you win, Jake," it read. "Play again?"

Jake moved the joystick to the "no" position. The Doomkritters logo filled the screen, flooding the room with an eerie green light. Finally, it presented them with their overall playing record as the doorbell rang. Taking his wallet from his pocket, Jim went to get the door and the delivery. Jake looked at the screen. The game didn't have enough memory to recount the number of games they'd played. Back when Jake was a kid, his dad had always beaten him. But as he got older, Jake won increasingly. Now his dad could only win in the first game or two, when his reflexes were not too slowed by the scotch he enjoyed so much. *Too much.*

Even so, the drinking was not a real problem. His dad was a gentle man who'd been defeated just after the market crash in October 1987. Until then, Jim and his grandfather had successfully run the company that marketed Doomkritters. But suddenly everything for the Carson family went horribly wrong.

When the market hit bottom, someone somehow had manipulated it so that the company could never rise again. His grandfather, Jeremy Carson, had a massive heart attack and drowned in his bath. Then, in a last-ditch attempt to rally the shareholders, Jake's father went to address a meeting of the only people who could pull the company out of the mire. But when he stepped up to the speaker's podium, his world fell apart.

As he began to speak, his vision clouded and his audience seemed to swim before his eyes. His head pounded and he panicked as flashes of violent color accompanied the terrifying sound of an animal screaming inside his head. Later, the psychiatrist explained the screaming he had heard was his own—he'd had a total mental breakdown in front of the shareholders he needed to impress.

That was years ago. Since then, his mental and financial recovery had been painful and slow. Finally, Jim gained enough strength to rejoin society, and now he managed a large accounting firm. The father and son lived comfortably, and alone. They rarely mentioned Jake's mother, Jasmine.

When things had gotten tough, Jasmine had simply packed her bags and left. Intent on rejuvenating a less than brilliant acting career, she made contact on Jake's birthdays and most Christmases. As far as they knew, she was still living with the TV newscaster she had met while Jim spent a month convalescing in the private sanitarium.

He had never had another attack, and the doctors were at a loss to explain the breakdown. The only thing they could liken it to was something they saw in patients who'd taken LSD, or similar hallucinogenic drugs. Yet Jim had never experimented with any drug—except alcohol. On the day of the fateful meeting, he'd had only a single glass of wine while lunching with one of the shareholders. The fear that such a breakdown could happen again was the thing that held him back and destroyed his confidence. "You've been spooked by this thing," his doctor explained. "It was likely a one-of-a-kind incident." But he refused to guarantee it would never recur.

Jake's father never drank before six o'clock at night. He never became aggressive or insensitive— just tired. Jake sensed there was a problem, but he knew his father put him first. The two enjoyed an easy live-and-let-live relationship.

"Dammit, why do they always put anchovies on their pizza!" Jake's father complained as he opened the carton.

"Told them not to," Jake said, "for the millionth time."

"Want another game after we eat?"

"I've got some homework. Plus a mystery disk to look at." Jim raised his eyebrows in a silent question. Jake took the three disks from his pocket. "I had two of these on the computer I use at school, but there was an extra one. Don't know which ones are mine—or what the other one is."

"Maybe if you got into the habit of labeling those things," Jim said with his mouth half full.

"Now you sound like Egghead Ol—the principal," Jake corrected himself.

"Well, you waste a lot of time if you don't," Jim said, turning on the news.

They finished eating and cleaned up, and Jake started for his room.

"Don't forget to clean your room. Your grandmother's coming in the morning."

"And don't forget to hide the scotch," Jake

teased, "or *your mother* will give her *little boy* another lecture."

"Get outta here." Jim laughed, and Jake left his dad to an evening of TV.

■Jake opened the door bearing the sign Chill Out or Keep Out! He walked into the room, carefully avoiding an Adidas track shoe, a sweatshirt, a pair of Speedo goggles, some weights, and several books. He used the uncluttered patches of carpet as stepping-stones to his own personal shrine—the computer desk. He'd clean up this mess later. Soon as he figured out which disk was which.

As he sat down and powered on the computer, he felt the cool evening breeze on his hand. Strange . . . his window was slightly open. He didn't remember unlocking it before he'd left for school. Must be losing it—he'd left the computer on at school and a window open here.

Outside, a dark-haired young man saw Jake's light come on. He frowned, started the yellow car, and drove away.

A few streets away in a darkened classroom, a man with a flashlight approached the school computer Jake had operated earlier that afternoon. As he flooded the workstation with light, he began to sweat. The disk was not where he'd left it! Trying not to panic, he zigzagged the surrounding area with the beam of light, double-checked, then checked again. Nothing! His trembling hand flicked off the flashlight. He took a deep breath. Then slowly, almost imperceptibly, he relaxed. A cruel smile shadowed his face. There was no time to lose —the plan must be activated immediately!

■ Jake slipped the third disk into the superdrive of the Power Mac. The first contained the assignment he had to finish for Monday; the second held data for the upcoming swimming carnival. He clicked the remaining disk into place and the head tapped for a few seconds as it read the ID. The disk icon appeared in the upper-right-hand corner of the screen and the word MUSIK appeared. He double-clicked the word; the computer made its distinctive tapping sound as the time icon spun. Soon, the contents of the disk were revealed. Four items came up. *Present, Past, Future,* and *Schedules.* Jake guessed it must contain some academic records for notes. For no particular reason he double-clicked *Schedules* first.

Again the computer drive tapped as it loaded. Suddenly a flood of letters and numbers filled the screen. Jake stared at it, puzzled. He scrolled through thousands of lines of numbers and letters. Each line followed a pattern similar to the first, which read:

C3E1A3 G3C2D2D3A2G1B2A3G3 B4E5F2B1
E1F3C1E1F2 E1C3E1C1D2B2G1

Oh no, thought Jake, *a code.* But he was excited. Cracking codes and hacking were a lot more fun than the spreadsheet operation covered in today's computer lab. But this code had something strangely familiar about it. Why did it remind him of the time he and some of the guys hacked into the army computer? Or was it the local government program where they uncovered the rezoning deal that forced a town planner to resign? Maybe he should ask his friends to help. Maybe they could remember. No, first he'd try and solve it himself.

He dumped everything onto the hard drive and began. He rapidly calculated that there were fifteen different units. That meant the code used more than just numbers, which needed just ten symbols. Must be a combination of numbers and letters. Or possibly letters alone. Okay. Usually the vowels recurred most frequently—so maybe E1 was a vowel, as it appeared four times. He initiated search and replace, trying each of the five vowels in succession. No pattern emerged. Okay, start again.

But two hours later he was no closer to a solution. He cracked his knuckles. He'd quit soon. The clock on his screen read 10:33 P.M. when his dad tapped on the door.

"I sure wouldn't want to be you when your grandmother sees this room tomorrow," Jim said. "You know what time it is?"

"Ten-thirty-three. No, make that ten-thirty-four. I'm quitting in a minute anyway."

"I sure hope so—I, for one, am turning in now. What time you want me to wake you up?"

"It's okay, I'll set the alarm. What time is Joyce the Voice coming?"

Jim suppressed a smile. "Your grandmother, if you don't mind, will be here around nine. So you

24

better get it together and be up and running by then."

"Okay," Jake reluctantly agreed as Jim left his room and closed the door. He stretched and looked out his window. The dog next door was attempting to wag her tail off as she greeted a returning neighbor. Across the street, someone turned off a lawn sprinkler. And a lonely cyclist passed the yellow car parked at the curb.

As Jake yawned and turned back to the computer screen, twin flashes of light glinted off the binoculars focused on his window.

■Old Redders couldn't sleep. Couldn't sleep at all. He'd done what he could to kill the pain—in fact, he'd gotten it to the point where he was just mildly uncomfortable. It wasn't the pain that kept him awake—it was just that he couldn't stop thinking.

Thinking how disastrous the fire could have been. And thinking about the things in the burned supply room.

At 10:45 P.M., he decided to go to work.

■As Jake tried to crack the computer code one more time, his father slept fitfully in the next room.

The nightmare Jim dreaded so much began. He was standing at a podium. But as he opened his mouth to speak, he began screaming uncontrollably. The audience stared at Jim in utter disbelief. Panicked, they fled from the meeting, overturning chairs as they raced toward the exits.

Except for one person. A distinguished-looking man, who calmly remained seated. He raised a half-filled wineglass to Jim in a toast and smiled as he deliberately dropped the glass to the floor. It smashed without a sound, and millions of crystal fragments floated through the air. Then the man pointed at Jim and started laughing. He laughed quietly at first, but his laughter became louder and louder. As it did, the man's mouth became larger and larger as it turned into a black cavern of menacing sound. Out of control, Jim was drawn into the noise and the darkness and began to fall through space. Faster and faster he fell, downward . . . downward . . . downward . . .

Fighting the dream as hard as he could, Jim finally succeeded in waking himself. He felt his heart pounding, his hair wet with perspiration. He fumbled for the bedside lamp and sighed as he took in the reality of the bedroom. He stumbled out of bed and into a dry T-shirt. He replaced his damp pillow with a fresh one. Now wide awake, he lay in bed thinking about the dream. This time he'd actually seen the man's face more clearly. He wondered if he'd ever recognize the man in the nightmare. And what—if anything—the dream might mean.

He considered the unfinished drink on his bedside table and took a few comforting sips. Then he turned out the light and slowly drifted into an uneasy sleep.

■ Jake was as irritable as he was tired. Nothing bothered him more than a video game he couldn't beat or a code he couldn't hack into. Well, maybe he *would* have to ask his friends to help tomorrow. He yawned again. His room still looked like a war game after final destruction. His grandmother was going to show up in less than eight hours. She'd want him to work all day, and he had six kids to teach in a diving class at 10:30—that meant he didn't have a hope of cracking this code till late tomorrow. Another thought crossed his mind: What if it was someone's personal information or something? What if it belonged to Egghead Oliver? —he was always in the lab—and what if he found out the young cop let Jake take the stuff? Then they'd both be in trouble. He decided he'd better get the disk back to where he'd found it first thing tomorrow. But tired as he was, he decided to make a copy—just to see if he could decode it. If it looked personal, he promised himself, he'd wipe it. Just a case of keeping a copy to try to hack the code. He fed the superdrive a fresh disk, formatted it, and dragged the musik icon across to overlap on the disk icon. The machine made its tapping sounds as the bar registering the portion of items copied moved from 0 to 100 percent. Jake left the copy in the drive and wrapped the original in his Speedos— just to make sure he'd remember to take it with him tomorrow. He'd go straight from the pool to the school on the way home. And get the disk back into the computer lab before anyone found it was missing. If it *was* Egghead Oliver's, he'd never know!

Groggily he returned to the computer and keyed

chapter three

"Martin, I wish you'd hurry up and come to bed—it's already after eleven-thirty."

"Just finishing my tea, dear," the principal called in the direction of the bedroom. But he knew he wouldn't sleep tonight. Finding a half-used hypodermic in that supply room had destroyed his day. And evening. He only hoped it wouldn't affect his future.

His wife, Anne, came downstairs pulling a robe on over a practical cotton nightdress. "You still worrying about that needle you found?"

"Well, I wish now that I'd pointed it out to the police instead of hiding it."

"Well, you didn't, and wishing doesn't change things. So take it from there."

He wished she wasn't so damned logical. "I realize that, dear," he said tersely. "But the point is, what should I do now? That hypodermic could've meant anything."

"Like what?"

"Well, it could simply be something that's not all that terrible. Like steroids. Some of the seventeen-year-olds got caught with them last year, remember?"

She yawned her reply. "So did a few athletes at Barcelona, remember?"

"Then again, it could be something—well, ominous. Like kids on hard drugs . . ." He shuddered. "And if something like that got out, it could spell disaster."

"For the students or your precious school?"

"Oh for God's sake, we didn't spend all those years building the best computer resource at a boys' school to see it wiped out by a scandal."

"Well, I'm sure you'll all be able to cover it up. That's the usual procedure around this place, isn't it?" She walked over to the liquor cabinet and poured herself a belt of sherry.

Anne was starting to annoy him. He knew exactly what she was referring to. She loved to bring it up again and again. And every time she did, he felt forced to explain his position to her. "You know there was nothing to be gained by telling anyone how Old Man Carson died."

"Thank you, *Egghead Oliver*." She raised her glass to him in a mock toast.

He noticed she'd almost emptied it.

"I have asked you a thousand times. Please stop referring to me as 'Egghead Oliver.'"

"Well, you act like a tired old academic these days—these years, come to think of it." She looked suddenly saddened. "Martin, I wonder if we'll ever find out what really happened to Jake's grandfather."

"Jeremy Carson's death may always contain some mystery—but I don't think it was the big cover-up you imagine. And I don't think anyone lied, either. He did have a heart problem—his doctor was expecting another major attack any moment."

"Was his doctor also expecting those marks they found on his neck? Like he'd been bitten by a shark or whatever it was . . ."

"A crocodile," he replied flatly.

"Yes, like he was bitten by a crocodile. While he was having a heart attack in a bathtub. In an innercity mansion. You all saw the evidence. Yet you all pretended it never happened."

Oliver was annoyed. "What possible good could it have done? The family had enough trouble as it was."

"And if probate on the will had taken too long, you might never have had your beloved computer lab when you did. It could have taken years to get the money he left the school. Let's not forget *that* little detail." By now she was really warming up. "And the last janitor at the school—he died of drugs. Another sudden death, right?"

"Mr. Hoskin was probably an addict—the police certainly thought so. Come to think of it, the needle I found may well have been one that he left behind and—"

"And of course the marks on his body just happened to match the ones they found on Jeremy Carson. And what happened? You all pretended they

31

didn't happen either. Your friend Max Pink kept the coroner well out of that one too. Well, the janitor didn't leave your precious school anything. So why the cover-up there? And why—"

"Why do you insist on bringing this up again and again?" he yelled at her. "What good does it do! You know how much damage these things can cause!"

"The damage has already been done," she said flatly. "Real damage. To you, Martin, for starters. And there's also the damage to *us* to consider. And maybe even to the boys who think you're honest and upright and—oh forget it." For a moment she was very quiet. "God, how I hate what we've become. Putting all these stupid machines, all this technology ahead of everything we believed in when we were young." Her face crumpled. "And sometimes I even hate myself. For going along with it. But most of all, for what it's done to us." Suddenly she felt unbelievably old and tired. Too tired even to try to change the unchangeable. Resigned, she said, "I'm sorry. I'm even beginning to bore myself now. I'm going to bed. Good night, Martin."

"Wait. You can't always start something and then walk away from the discussion. Just . . . tell me. What do you expect me to do?" He sounded desperate.

"You can do whatever you want. But I don't think it will matter now—things are way beyond our control."

"Meaning what?"

She shook her head. "Meaning I just have this

terrible feeling. That something absolutely awful will happen to someone. And it'll be our fault. Not because we did anything. But because we kept silent when we ought to have spoken out. Well, if something happens, something we could have helped prevent, I just wonder if we'll be able to live with ourselves."

As she turned to walk upstairs alone, Oliver thought how vulnerable she looked. And he wondered how they had allowed practicalities to take control of their lives. Well, maybe it wasn't too late to change things. To get back to the way they had been when they first met.

Maybe he *would* talk to Max Pink about the needle he'd concealed earlier. After all, he could trust Max to be discreet. Even better, he'd invite him fishing. Then, when the right moment came . . .

■ Max Pink drained his hot chocolate and placed the empty mug on the bedside table, beside his copy of the *Police Gazette* and his reading glasses. He rubbed the bridge of his nose where the glasses had made two small red ovals.

He'd sleep well tonight. But then he never had to count sheep. Even when things were chaotic at work, he could always relax. His men loved to tell new recruits about the time the chief attended the goriest car crash in the state's history. He'd been at the local McDonald's when the call came through on the radio. As he walked through the twisted wreckage and around the mutilated bodies and the blood, he saw the other officers fighting back nausea. But the chief just kept right on eating his two Big Macs and large order of fries. And followed them up with a chocolate shake.

But tonight was different. Tonight he was really perturbed. He'd known Martin Oliver now for decades, but he'd never seen him behave the way he had that afternoon. He had observed the principal cover something up with his right Florsheim loafer —something he didn't want the young officer, Lee —or him—to see. But what? He didn't mind his friends keeping secrets from his subordinates, but when they kept *him* in the dark too, well, that was real cause for concern. And then that stupid story about staying back to tie a shoelace. Loafers don't have shoelaces. Did Martin really think cops didn't notice those details? He was pretty sure Lee saw it too. But he didn't mention it. Why? Things like that worried Max. As much as he worried about anything.

Three minutes later he was snoring his head off.

■ Jake was having the most troubled sleep he'd had since the time his mother left home five years ago. He was at the bottom of an empty swimming pool. Trucks kept backing up to the pool and dumping tons of cubes on top of him. As soon as he could get out from under them, another load buried him. The cubes were like giant dice with letter-number symbols on their sides. Eventually there were too many for him to shift. Unable to move, he was trapped in a sea of numbers and letters reading C1, G3, E2, and dozens of other combinations he couldn't quite make out. He became aware of a pounding in his head. It got louder and louder, and as he drifted into consciousness he connected the pounding with someone hammering on his door. And someone was yelling too.

"It's after nine A.M., Jake. Are you there? Jake! Answer me, you hear?" The unmistakable voice of Joyce Carson.

Now awake, he felt terrible. His head ached. Like the time he had the Hong Kong flu that seemed to go on forever.

"I'm here, Grandma."

"You decent, then?"

"It's okay, I'm in bed. You can come in." Before he'd finished his invitation, his grandmother had barged in, talking at the top of her voice.

"Really Jake, I've been knocking on that door for five minutes"—that meant two, maximum—"and it's a perfectly lovely day and there are a lot of things to do around here, I can't possibly do everything myself. And just look at this mess! All these dirty clothes all over the floor and oooh," she added, sniffing the air, "this room smells like a grave." She marched to the window and hurled it open. "You really should leave this open at night— no fresh air, that's the trouble!"

Funny. He didn't remember closing the window. He remembered his father coming in, or *was* it his dad? Something about—

"Really, you're worse than your father was at your age." She continued talking as she picked clothing off the floor. "Of course it's not surprising, with no women in the house to keep things nice. Not that she understood how to run a house properly even when she *was* here."

"Oh Grandma, please . . ." Jake hated it when she started in on his mother.

But the voice continued to fill the background with sound as he tried to piece together the events of last night. He could remember working at the computer, trying to crack the code . . .

". . . very good at the *showy* food, but when it came to decent, well-balanced meals like I used to cook your father . . ."

Jake remembered something else. He'd just made a copy of the disk with the code, and he remembered putting it somewhere strange for some reason, but where?

"So I brought some homemade muesli this week and a couple of frozen casseroles that have everything in them and—well I must say, this is a strange place to put a computer disk," she said in answer to his unasked question. "Now, why would you wrap it in your bathing suit?" She extracted the disk from his Speedos and placed it on the workstation. "Your grandfather, bless his soul, knew more about computers than anyone else in this city will ever know. Invented Doomkritters all by himself. And *he* made a point of being organized with these things— course they were a decent size then—he always filed them away carefully. Why, I could've walked on it and ruined it and then where would you be. . . ."

He wished she'd stop so he could get out of bed. "It'd be okay, Grandma, it's not the only one—

there's a copy. It's still in the computer. Hey, you mind if I get up now?"

"For the life of me, I can't see what's stopping you—you seem to have gone to bed with all your clothes on. Well, I suppose that's a step in the right direction." She smiled at her little joke. Usually she complained that the new pajamas she bought him had never been worn. "I'm taking this stuff to the washer now," she announced, gathering the last of the dirty clothes. "When you finally get up, bring your sheets and pillowcases for me to wash as well." She swept out of the room, humming a few bars from "Dancing in the Dark."

Jake got out of bed and glanced in the mirror as he passed it. He was surprised to see he was still wearing the jeans and T-shirt from yesterday. But something just as unusual caught his eye. In all the time he'd had the computer, he had never closed the sliding shelf that held the mouse and keyboard. Puzzled, he pulled out the shelf and powered up. What he saw jolted him wide awake. All his files and programs had disappeared!

The voice reverberated through the house. "Where are those sheets, Jake? I'd really like to get this laundry done before noon."

"Yeah, yeah, right away, Grandma," he called back. As he did, he noticed the copy he'd made of the code disk was missing from his computer.

Too groggy to figure things out now, he started to strip the bed. But as he removed the bedding, he stopped dead. There was a red spot of dried blood on his pillowcase, about the size of a nickel. At the same time he felt a mild tingling sensation—like the time after a bee had stung him on that camping trip with his dad. He rubbed the tender spot and stared at the small bloodstain.

He was slowly piecing together the events of the previous evening. But the moments just before he'd fallen asleep were a mystery.

chapter four

The pain in his arm nudged Old Redders awake. He looked at his watch in disbelief. Half-past nine already! He remembered falling asleep in the janitor's room just after two in the morning. That was okay. He also remembered giving in again, and that was definitely not okay. He needed to hang on to this job, but it could ruin everything. Well, he'd gotten away with it yesterday, but next time he might not be so fortunate. He put his head in his hands and cursed the hypodermic lying on the table. He was lucky nobody had come in—or had they? No, the door was still bolted from his side. Trouble with drugs, they made things so unclear. Once again, he promised himself he'd be strong next time. With his pliers he snapped the hypodermic needle off its plastic barrel. He wrapped both parts in some old paint rags and buried the packet in the garbage compactor. Then he pushed the start button. The unit whirred and growled as it compressed the contents into a small undefined mass.

Old Redders relaxed. So far so good. Now he'd better do what he'd meant to do last night. He grabbed a handful of heavy-duty garbage bags and went to clean out the burned supply room.

■Jake's hands parted the cold water as he completed a perfect double somersault from the high board. His body flinched slightly as it reacted to the sudden change in temperature, then rapidly adjusted. For the first time since he woke up, he felt alive. He swam the length of the fifty-meter pool under water, then surfaced with air to spare. He felt just as secure in the water as he did in front of a computer. He flicked the water from his hair and butterflied back to the deep end with perfect form. His well-muscled arms eased his smooth swimmer's body up onto the pool surround. He peeled off his swim goggles and took a few deep breaths of the chlorine-laden air and stretched his shoulders. He checked out his new Seiko diving watch—a fifteenth-birthday present from his dad. Just ten minutes till the little sharks in his diving class started to show up. He stretched out and tried to unwind under the warm spring sun.

While his body relaxed, his mind raced. He'd gone over last night's events again and again. He knew something terrible had happened. He was almost certain he'd been drugged unconscious. Knocked out, and it had to be connected to the disk with the code. But whose disk was it, and why was it so important? He knew he was close to the answer. He knew all he had to do (*all!*) was crack the code. He started to plan. First, he had to reprogram the computer. Then he could pick up from where he'd left off last night. And he had another idea.

"What the—" He sat up with a jolt. Three ten-year-olds were laughing hysterically at his reaction. They'd managed to sneak up on him and drip cold water on his face. His pulse was racing and he was furious with them. He barked, "Okay, two laps right away, guys. Hurry up—last one back gets to do two more!" As they raced to the pool, Jake realized how uncool he'd been, how hyper this thing had made him. And he wondered if maybe he wasn't imagining things, making things out to be far worse than they really were.

■Old Redders pried the top off the can of Taubman's high-gloss enamel and looked at the contents. Everything was just as he'd left it. Half full, the paint had crusted over long ago. On top, a small cardboard box held the remainder of the drugs he hated himself for using yesterday. He was wrestling with his conscience and was on the verge of deciding to get rid of them once and for all when he heard footsteps coming down the hall. Soundlessly he replaced the cover of the paint can and placed it back on the shelf. He busied himself by sweeping the floor of the burned supply room when the owner of the footsteps stood in the doorway. Chief Max Pink.

"Little early for an injured man to be working isn't it." It was not a question, just one of those flat statements the chief loved to make. Old Redders hoped he didn't look as guilty as he felt.

"Gotta be done sometime, and it takes my mind off my arm," the janitor explained.

"Yeah. Well. Thought I'd better have a final look around. What happened to all the trash that was here?"

"Oh, it was a mess. Rags and cans and—all burned. Just shoveled it all up and got rid of it."

"That's the way." The chief smiled but his eyes were ice. "I guess you didn't find anything unusual in your cleanup?"

"I didn't go through things with a fine-tooth comb, that's for sure. But no, I didn't see anything —unusual, as you put it, Chief."

"Yeah. Well. I'll be going then. You take care of that arm now."

"Yes, sir. I will." Redders breathed a sigh of relief as the chief turned to go. But Pink suddenly stopped and turned. "The things you say you shoveled up and got rid of. How *do* you get rid of garbage around here? Incinerator? Compactor?"

Redders hesitated. "Compactor."

"Oh well. Probably not important anyway." And he left. Redder's pulse beat gradually slowed to normal as the chief's footsteps receded down the hallway.

■"Oh look, Heidi, Joyce's car is here." Lila Spooner was delighted at the chance to have one of her chats with her old friend. She opened the gate and led Heidi up the front steps.

Inside, Joyce was putting away her gardening gloves when she heard a noise from down the hall. "Jake," she called, "you home already?" She listened for an answer. "Jim, is that you, son?" No reply. "Hmmm," she murmured, assuming she'd been mistaken. She started to fill the kettle when she heard the front doorbell. Wiping her hands on her apron, she marched to the door. "Be right there."

As Lila rang the doorbell, she heard a sound at the side of the house. She walked across the verandah and peered between the Carsons' house and the neighboring bungalow. Heidi started barking as Lila saw a dark-haired young man running away. He glanced backward, and for the briefest moment, he and Lila made eye contact. Joyce opened the front door. "Lila, what's the commotion?"

Lila pointed excitedly at the disappearing figure. "Over here, Joyce. Hurry!" Then, "Oh, you're too late—he's gone already."

"Who's gone?"

"The one I saw at the fire. He was running away then too."

"I don't understand what you're talking about. Anyway, tell me about it over a cup of tea. I need the break—at least my knees do. I've just been planting petunias."

"Yes, I noticed." Lila took another look between the houses for good measure. "He's well gone, now." She followed Joyce into the house. By the time they got to the kitchen she'd told her about the young man she'd seen running from the fire. "And I know it's the same one I saw just now."

"Well, I *thought* I heard a noise from Jake's room," Joyce said thoughtfully. "Oh, probably he was one of Jake's friends. Tapping on his window. They do that sometimes. Though it's usually late at night when they're afraid to wake up the whole house."

"No, he was up to no good. I can tell. And this time I got a real good look at him. I'd recognize those eyes anywhere." She nodded vigorously. "Oh, I'll know him next time all right. *Then* we'll see what our rude chief of police has to say."

Joyce humored her. "Do you think I should call them?"

"It won't do a bit of good. They only care about solving crimes, not preventing them. Well, you're lucky he didn't steal your son's VCR, or Jake's—"

"Look, I'm sure it was just one of Jake's friends," Joyce interrupted. And because she was bored she changed the subject. "Have you seen that Chinese cooking show?" She launched into a long description of the young chef, his recipes, where she found the ingredients.

Lila lost track of the conversation, but as she sipped her tea she appeared fascinated and nodded at the right moments. She deferred to Joyce, even though Joyce had lost her husband and the bulk of the family fortune. But old habits die hard, and Lila was happy to be a friend.

Joyce, on the other hand, saw Lila as an endless source of information. And because Lila deferred to her, Joyce rather liked having Lila around. Even if she was more of a henchperson than friend.

Lila waited for a suitable gap in the monologue and seized the opportunity. "By the way, your grandson was rather rude to me at that fire." She told Joyce how Jake had nearly run her down, how he almost insulted her.

It was a mistake. Whatever differences Joyce had with her son and her grandson, no one outside the family should dare to criticize. Joyce's smile had a certain edge. "You know, my dear, you shouldn't step onto the roads without looking. Roads are mainly for the use of vehicles after all. And of course bicycles are especially dangerous, often hard to hear," she added for good measure, "especially as we grow older, don't you think?"

Lila nodded her agreement. She hated it when Joyce did this. Made her feel so old. And there were only months between them. Well, that's what money did. Joyce hadn't ever worked until a few years back. Lila decided to change to a subject they both agreed on. "I don't suppose you've seen that cake mix commercial? It's running again."

"Of course I have," Joyce answered sharply. "Well, they got the right person for it all right. Jasmine never could make a cake from scratch. Not one you'd care to eat, anyway. And the way they make her look like the perfect mother. Smiling and laughing and hugging the children. Playacting the mother, just like she did with Jake. Hunh! They should have a movie of me doing all the things around here that she should have been doing!"

"Nobody believes those ads anyway. I hear she's gone overseas."

"She sent Jake a birthday card from London. Living with a cameraman apparently."

"I thought she was engaged to a director."

"That was the one before. I guess she must be coming down in the world."

"I'm not surprised. What did Jake think?"

"Hard to say, really. He's so independent. He still sticks up for her. Lord knows why, the way she carried on. But he and his father seem to manage all right—with a little help from yours truly." She waited for the compliment. Lila gave in.

"I always say I don't know how Joyce does it. Running two houses at once, really. Did you ever think about living together—the three of you?"

"Jim suggested it once, but no, it wouldn't work. Jim ought to have a stable relationship—marry someone decent this time. And Jake—well, it'd be nice if he had someone more like a mother in the house. Even if he's only at home a few more years. But no, that would never happen if I moved in."

"Two women in a house is one too many, I always say," Lila offered.

"Anyway," Joyce spoke in a confidential tone, "I have a feeling that Jim is *very* interested in someone —an extremely suitable person."

"Who?"

"Well, that's really not for me to say. Not that

you'd know her anyway. She's very *social*. Adelaide family—a young widow."

Lila hated the way Joyce rubbed it in—telling her she wouldn't know anyone social. She nudged the sleeping dachshund with her foot. Heidi growled. "Oh dear, sounds like my baby needs some fresh air. Come on then, Heidi. Well, thanks for the tea, dear."

"My pleasure." Joyce didn't like it when Lila was the one to end a visit. The two women and the dog walked to the door and parted the way they always did, pleasant on the surface but inwardly irritable. Joyce closed the door and Lila muttered under her breath, "Not social indeed!" As she stopped to get the gate, Heidi squatted over one of the petunias Joyce had just planted, and peed.

"Good girl," Lila whispered, and led the dachshund away.

■Jake was exhausted. Whatever had happened to him last night made today's diving class sheer hell. As he toweled himself dry, one of his kids came up to him. "Are you really mad at us, Jake? We were just having fun."

"It's okay, just had a late night. You know, homework and stuff," he lied.

"Yeah?"

"Tell you what. We'll check out McDonald's and share a few orders of fries."

"Just a few between all of us?"

"Come on, you're supposed to be going home for your lunch now. Your parents'll kill me anyway," Jake laughed. Then he added a threat. "Course, if you don't think it's worth going for—"

"You kidding? I'll tell the others."

The bicycle convoy descended on the McDonald's parking lot. As his diving class attacked the rations, Jake thought the term "fast food" ought to describe the way kids ate. In minutes they'd devoured everything. As they went their separate ways, Jake was glad he'd treated them. The money he earned teaching them came in real handy. Besides, it wasn't *their* fault he was so edgy. The thought brought him back to reality. So whose fault was it then?

■ Max Pink was in a foul mood. Here it was approaching lunchtime, and he was starving. His day had started in the worst possible way—with a 6 A.M. telephone call from the States. Didn't they know it was Saturday here? Didn't they know how early it was?

They'd ruined his day off, his breakfast, and now lunchtime was being jeopardized. Two years to retirement. Then no more responsibility. Better yet, there'd be no more contact with sleazy criminals, no more smiling at a bunch of kids to convince them the police were their best friends. And best of all, no more shitty jobs like this—poking around in garbage compactors and transferring the contents into the neatly labeled plastic bags. And why he wasn't to let anyone help, he simply didn't understand. Still, the orders came from so high up there was no point in questioning. He collected the last bag and placed it in the trunk of the squad car. Unseen, Old Redders watched the chief drive off with the contents of the compactor.

■Jake parked his bicycle in the usual place and ran into the house. "I'm home, Grandma. What's for lunch?" As he went into the kitchen he saw a note from Joyce on the table.

> *Jake:*
> *Your father called. Said to tell you he'll be home late—around eight. I've gone to Woolies to get more oven cleaner (and I sure hope they sell it in ten-quart packs!!!). Eat all your lunch.*
>
> *Love, Grandma*

Her note reminded Jake of the casserole that boiled over the night he and his dad got absorbed in an extra tie-breaker game of Doomkritters. Well, she couldn't be too mad—the note was signed "Love, Grandma." When she was really annoyed she signed things "Your Grandmother, Joyce Carson."

Jake wolfed down the nutritionally correct whole-grain tuna salad sandwich and carrot juice she'd left in the fridge. Then he went to his room. He powered up the computer and snapped on his small black and white TV. Thank God for *The SatAft Rockshow*. It ought to help kill time while he reloaded everything onto the hard drive.

The host bounced onto the screen. Another forty-year-old with a hair transplant acting *groovy*. Still, he always got the best acts. Today one of Jake's favorite groups, Fraylex, was promoting its new CD and playing the title track for the first time. "And after that," enthused the host, "we have an exclusive interview with Brian Croffert—the keyboard genius in this group of totally awesome Aussies!" He flashed several thousand dollars' worth of dental work at the camera as the studio audience joined the canned applause. Then the group began to play.

"Does that have to be so *loud*?" demanded the loudest voice in Jake's life. He turned around to see Joyce with a cloth in one hand and a can of Mr. Sheen in the other.

"Hi, Grandma, thanks for lunch. Uh—I know we forgot to clean out the oven. Sorry about that."

"Well, never mind, men are never *totally* domesticated. What you really need around here is a woman's touch—on a regular basis too." She nodded knowingly. Jake knew she was getting at something, but what? He only hoped she wasn't planning to move in.

"Oh," she said, cleaning the windowsill, "I'm pleased to see you opened a window. This room is usually gasping for oxygen."

"I didn't open it."

"Well, then, I don't know who did. I made sure everything was shut before I went shopping."

Jake wished his grandmother would leave him alone. "Maybe I did open the window, Grandma— must have been on autopilot."

Joyce looked baffled. "Well, I have a few more things to do here. And so do you. Though how you use a computer with that TV blaring away I don't know. When your grandfather was inventing

Doomkritters, he insisted on total silence for his concentration. Wouldn't allow anyone to speak a word—not even *me*. Imagine! Of course Australia's gotten so noisy lately, well, I doubt anyone in the country could even invent a game like Doomkritters today. Unless maybe they originally came from Japan," she added, leaving the room. Jake returned to the task of reloading his computer. Alone at last.

■Someone was monitoring Jake's progress. In the school's computer lab, every keystroke he entered appeared simultaneously on another screen.

■"Finally," Jake muttered to himself. Everything was reloaded and things were back to normal—at least as far as the computer was concerned. Jake inserted the code disk into the superdrive and watched thoughtfully as the strange groupings reappeared on the screen. He was pondering one combination, E1F3C1E1F2, when the *Rockshow* host started the interview with Fraylex's keyboard genius, Brian Croffert.

"Now, Brian," the host said, "you say you have every drum sound on the keyboard. Can you tell the fans how this works?"

"Yeah, man. See, I put the bass drum on C1, the snare on E2 and the toms on D3 to A3. Then—"

"Hold on a minute, you've lost me. What are all these strange numbers you're referring to?"

"Oh yeah. Well, the keyboard is a series of octaves. Octave 1, octave 2, octave 3, and so on. Each octave has seven basic notes—like C, D, E, F, G, and A. So C1 is the first note on the keyboard, D1 is the second, and so on. So it's just like—um—a location map, so to speak."

"I see," the host said unconvincingly. "Does this mean it's like a—a musical alphabet?"

"You got it, man—it's a code that lets the keyboard MIDI with other instruments or a computer, see."

In the studio, the host beamed. In his room, Jake felt the blood drain from his face and a tingling in his scalp. He was oblivious to the rest of the interview. The code on his screen was beginning to make sense. Suddenly he understood—he was looking at either a piece of music or a new way of writing the alphabet. One thing he was absolutely certain of—he'd soon know what this strange disk was all about. He listed the notes in their keyboard sequence. "Okay," he muttered to himself as he typed, "he said C1 was the first key. So let's assume the first key equals the first letter of the alphabet. That makes C1 the same as the letter A. The next key is D1, so I'll call that letter B. E1 follows, so it's letter C and . . ." He continued with the progression. Ten minutes later he'd charted a keycode. The screen read:

C1	D1	E1	F1	G1	A1	B1	C2	D2	E2	F2	G2	A2
A	B	C	D	E	F	G	H	I	J	K	L	M

B2	C3	D3	E3	F3	G3	A3	B3	C4	D4	E4	F4	G4
N	O	P	Q	R	S	T	U	V	W	X	Y	Z

The man monitoring Jake's progress watched in disbelief as his screen told him exactly what Jake had discovered. His face contorted with rage as he slammed a trembling hand onto the table.

"Bloody hell! He's in." The violence of his own reaction frightened him. But he knew it was time to call in a few favors. He reached for the phone.

■ Jake took a deep breath and crossed his fingers for a moment. He was ready to find out if his hunch was right. To see if his code worked, he selected a group of symbols from the document at random. He chose E1C3E1C1D2B2G1. Then he translated the symbols into the alphabet letters of his code key. It was a word all right—a word that sent shivers down his spine: COCAINE.

"Well, I'm off now," boomed the voice. Jake jumped.

"I didn't hear you come in, Grandma."

"My, my, we *are* nervous, aren't we," Joyce observed. "What on earth is wrong with you today, you seem so . . . jumpy?"

"I don't know. I had a strange experience last night and now things are—like really weird. Grandma, what would you say if I told you I thought someone came in here last night and wiped everything off my computer?"

"I'd say you ought to get more sleep and stop imagining things," she said. "I certainly hope you haven't inherited *her* characteristics—she was always so unstable, forever talking about things that never happened, causing scenes over nothing at all." Jake was wincing as Joyce fixed him with a stare. "What time did you finally turn in last night?"

"Pretty late, I guess."

"There you are. You can't stay up playing with that thing forever and expect to live a normal life. Now, if you take my advice, you'll get a good night's sleep tonight and be right as rain in the morning. Okay?"

"I—I guess so. Well, thanks for doing everything today." He got up and gave her a hug. "You really are good to us, Grandma."

She gave him an affectionate smile. "It's my pleasure. You and your father are all I've got, you know. Oh! When he gets home, tell him the office called —something about a meeting in Cairns, and to call the secretary. No matter how late. Be sure and tell him, must be very important seeing as how it's a weekend and all. Well, I'd better be going, tonight's my bridge night. See ya."

"See ya," he echoed.

He heard the front door slam. Maybe she was right after all. Computers crash, things happen. And the word *cocaine*. Maybe it was just part of a story or something. Well, there was only one way to find out. Translate more of the document. He loaded a complex search-and-replace program and started entering equivalents. Once that was done, he'd be able to get a translation of the whole mysterious disk in less than a minute. He began to enter a set of instructions into his computer: Find C1. Replace with

A. Find D1. Replace with B. Find E1. Replace with C. Find . . .

As he loaded information robotically, he wondered if his grandmother had always been so loud. Hey, maybe his granddad had been a bit deaf. He smiled at the idea. It was hard to imagine Joyce the Voice ever being different. And yet, in that picture with Granddad by the old plane, they both looked so young and glamorous—even if it was only in an old movie kind of way.

chapter five

The Lockheed Constellation taxied laboriously down the runway and came to a dignified stop outside the terminal. To twenty-five-year-old Jeremy Carson it was the most incredible aircraft he'd ever seen.

"Look at *that*, Joycie—isn't she beautiful!" He couldn't take his eyes off the dolphinlike aircraft with the triple tailfins.

"I guess so, but I still feel nervous," she said, picking the remaining confetti from her hair. "Gee, I wish everyone had thrown rice, I feel like a sideshow." People were in fact looking at the pretty young bride mainly to see where the loud voice was coming from.

He put his arm around her and smiled. "Anyone as lovely as you are can steal any show. Any time."

"Oh Jeremy." She still melted whenever he paid her a compliment. "When do you think we'll be in London?"

"Darling, this is just about the fastest passenger

56

plane in the world. Just two nights in the air, a night in Singapore, and one in Cairo. Then, before we know it, we'll be in London. All up, less than four days—imagine!"

"Must be fast all right."

"Around three hundred miles an hour."

"I still can't help feeling nervous—I keep thinking about the *Titanic*. After all, this is a maiden flight."

"In more ways than one."

"Jeremy! Don't be so naughty." She was blushing.

"Aw, c'mon, it'll be super. Other airlines have been flying these babies all over the world for quite a while now. They're so darned popular we're even thinking about putting out a toy version—if we can get the rights from Lockheed and—looks like it's time to go on board." He kissed her on the cheek, and they went to join the other twenty-seven passengers boarding the *Charles Kingsford Smith* that balmy December evening.

■Halfway between the Australian coastline and Singapore, Joyce was idly looking through the *Australian Women's Weekly* when a distinguished-looking young man about Jeremy's age walked down the narrow aisle toward the rest room. As he passed them, the plane hit a turbulent patch of air. The aircraft fell about a hundred feet, and he was suddenly flung in Joyce's direction. *"Mein Gott,"* he exclaimed as he landed in the aisle beside her.

"Are you all right?" Joyce said, looking down from her leather-upholstered seat.

"I—I think so," the man replied, and braced himself against another bump. "But you look terrified."

"She's not too enthusiastic about flying yet," Jeremy told the man, talking across the ashen-faced Joyce. "It's okay, Joycie," he told her, "just a little bumpy air." Then to the man. "Her first flight."

"Oh." He smiled. "Well, it's no bumpier than the roads are where I come from—in far North Queensland," he added as he got up. The turbulence seemed to have stopped. "I'm Jan Mulder," he told Joyce, and Jeremy introduced himself and his bride. They all shook hands. "Why don't we go back and have a drink?" Jan suggested. "It'll take your mind off things and settle your stomach."

■ Half an hour and a few brandies later, the three were chattering happily. Jan told them how he'd been one of the fortunate Jews who'd escaped early in the war. He'd come to Australia and managed to take over an unsuccessful Cairns tin mine. Now that its success was assured, he wanted to branch out into manufacturing children's products, "To take advantage of the baby boom that's bound to follow."

"That's a coincidence—our family's been in toys since the twenties," Jeremy told him. "And after a week of honeymooning in London, we're going over to Amsterdam for the international toy fair. Maybe even bring back some new ideas."

58

"This must be a night for coincidences." Jan smiled. "I'm going to the same exhibition. But I really want to investigate television. It's going to be big—bigger even than radio, perhaps."

"I've never seen television, though I'm looking forward to it. But what makes you so sure it's not just another novelty? I mean, even the head of 20th Century–Fox said people will get tired of staring at plywood boxes every night."

"Ah yes. I read that too. But people also predicted man could never fly and"—he shrugged his shoulders and smiled—"look at us now—twenty-five thousand feet above the ground."

"It's much too far off the ground as far as I'm concerned," said Joyce. Jeremy smiled at her and patted her hand before turning back to Jan.

"Well, say television isn't just a novelty, and say it does last, what can it possibly have to do with children's products?" Jeremy was puzzled.

"Nothing, perhaps. But"—Jan was suddenly intense as he spoke slowly and deliberately—"I have this strong feeling that the two might go together somehow." Then he closed the conversation. "But that's a topic I'd like to be more wide awake to discuss."

He rose to leave. "If we're in Amsterdam at the same time, look me up. I'm staying at the Krasnapolsky."

"We're booked in the same hotel, but I'm not sure when we get there—"

"We arrive on December twelfth," Joyce volunteered.

"I will buy you a drink then in honor of our reunion. But now if you'll excuse me, I think I'll try and see if I can catch a little shut-eye. And I must say, Joyce, you look relaxed enough to sleep as well."

"The brandy helped." She stifled a yawn and looked around the cabin. "Gee, we seem to be the only people awake—except for the stewards. And I really *am* tired."

"Getting married is very exhausting—or so they tell me, I've yet to try it. Well, pleasant dreams, now." He walked back to his seat thinking the charming young bride had the loudest voice he'd ever heard in his life. Even the drone of the Constellation's four Curtis-Wright engines failed to suppress a single syllable she uttered!

"What a fascinating guy," Jeremy said as soon as Jan was out of earshot.

"Continentals are so cultured, aren't they!" Joyce enthused. "I'm really looking forward to Europe."

"*And* the Raffles Hotel bridal suite in Singapore," Jeremy said.

Joyce blushed again.

■An hour out of Singapore the Constellation encountered enough turbulence to jolt Jan wide awake. He was grateful for the reality. He'd been dreaming again about the operating theater in the concentration camp. He had watched as the young neurosurgeon inserted another electrical probe into the hypothalamus of his patient's brain. No anesthetic had been administered, and the patient's head was clamped firmly in a stainless steel vise, the body secured to the narrow table with wide leather straps. As he switched on the electrical current, the screaming began. Undeterred, the doctor began moving the probe in various directions and dictating notes to an assistant. Jan still sweated as he recalled the patient's face contorting in agony, the screaming growing louder and louder, the body convulsing in unimaginable pain. After several minutes the surgeon reluctantly ordered the current to be cut. He withdrew the probes. "*Still* not accurate enough," he said irritably. Peeling off his surgical gloves, he left the theater. "We'll try again later. Now clean the bastard up."

"We'll be landing in Singapore in another hour, sir. Can I get something for you?" The steward's voice cut across Jan's thoughts.

"I'm not hungry. But a cup of tea would be nice, thank you."

"Right away, sir. Incidentally, the captain tells us the weather in Singapore is extremely comfortable today. Considering the time of year, we're very fortunate."

"Yes, very fortunate."

Jan smiled ironically as the steward went for the tea. *Fortunate meant more than fair weather, witless airborne butler! Fortunate meant getting out of Germany in time and coming to Australia. Fortunate meant getting enough money from the party to buy a perfect cover—the business in Queensland. But most of*

61

all, fortunate meant having a place to continue the experiments . . .

"Here's your tea, sir. Milk and sugar?"

"I prefer it with just lemon, steward."

"A man after my own heart, sir. I fancy things a bit tart myself."

"I dare say." Jan turned to study the cumulus clouds framed in the circular window.

14 December 1947
Amsterdam: two weeks later

"And this one is called the Herengracht." Jan was explaining the network of canals that both divided and unified Amsterdam. "Walk a bit farther and we're in the Dam. And our hotel."

"I'll be glad to get out of the cold." Joyce's voice echoed off the frozen cobbled streets. "You and Jeremy can talk about business, but I'm going up to our room for a hot bubble bath."

"You can tell the honeymoon's over," Jeremy teased. "She can't wait to be alone." Joyce was too cold to blush.

"We're still having dinner though. My treat, remember?" Jan reminded them.

"Oh yes," Joyce enthused, "I'll be warm enough for cold champagne by then!"

Joyce went up to their room, and the men went to the bar and ordered brandies. After they'd discussed their tennis games in Singapore, the rooms at Raffles, and the disastrous stopover in India, they turned to talk of the future. "I agree with you about both things," Jeremy said. "Television is really impressive, and it's got to be in every home—as you say, just like radio is today. And I also agree kids' toys are in for a big change, but . . ."

"But you still can't see how toys and television will go together."

"No, not really. And you haven't really explained it, old boy."

Jan laughed. "These strange English expressions sound even stranger in Australian accents. Imagine —two young men calling each other 'old boy.'" He shook his head, laughing.

"I guess it does sound crazy. But look old—Jan, if you do ever put the two together, talk to me first, will you? We can always use a hot idea."

"Jeremy, I don't think it will happen tomorrow, or maybe even next year. But I do have an idea, barely formed, perhaps, but one I feel is possible. I can see a game where players push buttons and make things move on the screen. A game where they compete with something that's already on the screen. So perhaps it may happen in two, four, six, who knows how many years. But if I come up with an idea first—"

"You'll give it to us?"

"I'm not that generous, *old boy*."

"I asked for that. I meant, will you give us the first chance to put it on the shelves—for a really good deal, I mean?"

"I promise to talk to you first. Let's shake on it.

Now, we'd both better freshen up, or your bride will think we're ignoring her like we did in Singapore."

"That tennis club was impossible to leave, wasn't it though."

"So embarrassing to be beaten on one of the world's best courts! Never mind. One day we'll have a return match and you'll see a European triumph!"

"Any time. Well, see you in the dining room."

■Joyce thought the dinner was a perfect end to a wonderful two weeks. Jan had business in Europe that, he said, would keep him away from Australia until March. Joyce and Jeremy told him of their plans for an Australian Christmas in their Blue Mountains cottage. They agreed to get together in a few months, but somehow it was to be years before they would meet again. As they left the restaurant, an ugly incident occurred—one that took the edge off what had been a perfect evening.

A distraught-looking woman walked purposefully up to the trio as they were saying their farewells. She was short, almost skeletal, and her haunted eyes had dark circles under them. "You don't remember me, *Doktor,* do you!" she spat at Jan. He wheeled to face her, the color draining from his face. Joyce thought she saw recognition there, but she wasn't certain.

"I'm sorry, madam. You must be mistaken, I am not a doctor."

"Not now, perhaps, but you were a doctor where

I got this!" She peeled up the shabby sleeve of her coat to reveal a concentration camp tattoo on her left wrist. Jeremy noticed that its number ended in 339. "You watched them put the electrodes in my mother's brain, while she was wide awake! You're the one that turned the current on for your filthy experiments! You cut her skull open, while she was *wide awake*! Nazi murderer!" By now she was screaming and beating Jan's body with her clenched fists. She tried to claw his face, but he turned away. Not fast enough. One of her nails scratched his cheek deep enough to draw blood. The hotel staff moved in quickly. The crowd that had gathered was well dressed. Instinctively they saw Jan as one of them. Therefore, she was the enemy, the intruder, the outsider—these judgments are made in moments. The hotel security dragged her away. "Nazi monster! You killed my mother!" She broke down sobbing. "My beautiful mother. She was so kind, and . . . now we can never hold her . . . never hold her again."

Any remaining doubts about Jan were dispelled immediately as Joyce spoke. "Why didn't you tell her you're Jewish too? Why didn't you say you were in Australia during the war? Why, Jan, why didn't you?"

"I—I don't know, I was surprised. It's all so unexpected and—improbable. Poor woman." He put a handkerchief to where she'd scratched him and drawn blood. "She must be deranged. The casualties of war." He shrugged helplessly and the crowd dispersed.

■Later, Jeremy and Joyce lay in bed recalling the turbulent events of the evening. "Joyce, do you think there's anything strange about Jan?"

"No, it was just a terrible misunderstanding." She lay quiet for a while. "Why, do *you* think there's anything strange?"

"I guess not, it's just that he isn't a typical Jew, I don't think."

"How do you mean?"

"Well, after we played tennis in Singapore we had a shower, and I couldn't help noticing. Jan isn't circumcised."

"Oh," Joyce said. But she was simply puzzled.

■That night, in a double bed in the Hotel Krasnapolsky, Jake's father, Jim Carson, was conceived.

■That same night, in a different room in the same hotel, a brilliant idea was conceived. Jan Mulder devised the first video game as we know it today.

■That same night, in sight of the same hotel, all this unbridled conception was balanced by violent death. The body of a young Jewish woman, her head crushed beyond recognition, was found floating in the Herengracht. Police observed that her left wrist had been tattooed with numbers. The last three read 339.

chapter six

the present

". . . and find G4 replace with . . . Z. Done!"

"You always talk to yourself now?"

Jake jumped. "Dad, I didn't hear you come in."

"Sorry. What happened to the teenager with nerves of steel?"

"Superkid is cracking a code, Dad."

"Yeah? Sorry I'm late. Visit went on longer than I planned. Your grandmother okay today?"

"A bit pissed off about the oven being so dirty, but, yeah, mostly she was cool."

"Uh huh. Anyone call?"

"Oh yeah. You're supposed to phone your secretary."

"Not on a Saturday night—I want to live a bit longer, thanks."

"That was the message: Call when you get in, no matter how late."

"Strange, guess I better do it right away. You got her on your communications program there?"

"Aw, Dad, I was just about to crack this code."

"That computer is—"

"I know, technically yours. Okay, okay. I'll bring it up."

He invoked the communications package and highlighted Sarah's line. He clicked the mouse, and the computer autodialed.

"You want private?" Jake asked over the ringing tone.

"Speakerphone's fine," Jim said.

"Sarah Perkins, here." It was, Jake thought, the voice of someone who never had fun. It was, Jim knew, the voice of someone whose only fun was being sarcastic. "Sarah, sorry to call you at home but—"

"Thank heavens you did. Mr. Carruthers keeps checking on whether or not I got you. This is the story . . . Nufenix Corporation in Cairns . . ."

"*The* Nufenix Corporation . . ."

"Well, of course, how many can there be?" Sarah sounded irritable. "Anyway, Mr. Carruthers has been trying for years to get their business. The managing director is apparently very eccentric. He's agreed to transfer everything to the firm—" Jim whistled in amazement. She ignored the intrusion. "Provided he can have a meeting with you tomorrow. In Cairns."

"I can't get to Cair—"

"Of course you can. Anyone can. See, there are these things called airplanes, and they take people to Cairns all the time, Jim. Anyway, Mr. Carruthers expects it. In any event, it's only for a short meeting, and then you can come right back. Thing is, the Nufenix people want some advice before they fly out to Germany later in the day. Now, here's a mobile number. When you arrive at Cairns airport the chauffeur will collect you."

"But how am I supposed to know who—"

She sniggered. "I gave them a perfect description of you."

He shuddered to think of her choice of words. "What about booking the flights and—"

"I am not a travel agent, Jim. I am a personal secretary. But guess what, there are these books called the yellow pages. Now, under the letter A . . ."

"Yeah, Sarah. Airlines. I'll do it."

"And when you get your flights organized, leave the numbers on my answering machine, and I'll make sure the information is passed along."

"You going out?"

"No, but this is enough office work—too much office work, in fact—for a Saturday."

"Have a wonderful weekend, then." He motioned for Jake to disconnect.

"Now to get to Cairns and back. You've got AeroRez on line?"

"Yes sir." Jake loaded the program and tapped into the airline's booking service. The flights for Sunday were wide open. He booked Jim out on TN21 at 9:10 A.M. "That gets you to Cairns at eleven-oh-five, and let's see, there's something back at three-thirty, gets you home tomorrow at eight-twenty. Trouble is you have to make a connection at Brisbane."

"Anything better?"

"The program always gives you the most efficient available. Book it?"

Jim nodded and Jake clicked "OK."

The program asked for a credit card number. Jim read the numbers as Jake entered them. As Jake entered the confidential code, it came up onscreen as ****. The message "Transaction approved" appeared, followed by an authorization number. The program closed with the advice to "claim ticket at airport half hour prior to departure time."

"Done," Jake said and pressed control P. The printer spat out the details.

"Beats dealing with Sarah, I guess," Jim said as he folded the printout and pocketed it. "I'm going to fix myself a scotch, then how about a game of guess what?"

"Not Doomkritters again . . . I want to crack this code."

"Well, work on whatever it is, then we can play before we eat." And he left Jake to his project—another of Egghead Oliver's weird assignments, he imagined.

■ For the first time, the man monitoring Jake's progress smiled. Very good, very good indeed. At least this part was running exactly to plan. But he frowned as AeroRez was closed and the search-and-replace program reopened.

■ The police were working late. Pink hated it. He was convinced his stomach was grumbling loud

70

enough to get a 10 on the Richter scale. And smelling this garbage when you're thinking about hamburgers. Jeez!

The forensic man they called "The Prof" had been sent over to help see if the carefully cataloged bags from the school compactor contained anything of interest. The chief and his young officer had sat and watched as the Prof continued picking through the garbage with the meticulous dedication of an archaeologist. The three had been in the tiny lab room for nearly two hours with no result when the Prof attacked the specimen bag labeled 9209C1420. As he separated the tangled layers that included a plastic Coke bottle, a couple of paint-can lids, and a turpentine-soaked rag, something caught the chief's anxious eye.

"Hey, what's that?"

"Looks interesting, Chief. This what you're after?" He held up a crushed hypodermic barrel in his dirtied stainless steel forceps. "Still a drop of fluid in it too."

"Should tell us lots. But what are the odds of getting prints off it?"

"Not a snowflake's," the Prof replied. "Naturally we'll try, but . . ."

"Probably a waste of time. Just see what's inside."

"That's an easy one." The Prof seemed disappointed the search was over. "I'll try for prints anyway, but . . ."

"I'll be back for it in half an hour—if you figure that gives you enough time."

"Piece of cake. Could even be sooner." He was feeling extra helpful. "The minute I get something I'll bring it down to your office."

"You better keep it here for us, Prof." Pink smiled as he started to leave the room. "Right now Lee and I have an appointment at Cooper Road Station."

The Prof looked puzzled. "I didn't know the department had an office in—"

As he followed the chief from the room, Lee explained. "McDonald's. Ya want something?"

"No thanks, I got yogurt."

■ "Would *sir* care for more linguine?"

Martin Oliver nodded. "I must say, you're in an unusually playful mood, my dear."

Anne shrugged. "God knows why, but I had a wonderful sleep last night. Maybe we should argue about withholding evidence more often."

"Think I'll pass on that one. The idea kept me awake for ages."

"Pangs of conscience at this stage of life?"

He was suddenly in no mood to banter. "Pangs of panic is more like it. I'm terrified in case you've intuitively put your finger on something."

"My prediction of impending doom, you mean?"

"Mmm. Start adding things up and they don't exactly point to a happy ending. I mean, beginning with Old Jeremy Carson's suicide in eighty-seven— if it *was* suicide."

"The marks on his neck?"

"Exactly. How are they connected with similar marks on the previous janitor's neck?"

"The junkie janitor . . ."

"If he was. It just doesn't seem to fit. And that needle in the supply room fire. I wish I hadn't been there. Maybe we'd know what it was about."

"Martin, I want to say something, and please promise you won't snap at me."

"Only fools make blind promises. But I'll try."

"Why don't you talk to Max Pink? Before something happens. I'm not paranoid—well, no more than usual—but suppose there *is* something strange happening. You could be in danger. I mean, you have evidence that could implicate someone. If they knew you had . . ."

Martin's eyes widened abruptly.

"What is it?"

"The yellow car—"

"What yellow car?"

"Maybe I'm *becoming* paranoid, but yesterday when I went to see Old Redders at the hospital, this yellow car practically ran me down. I had a feeling in the back of my mind it'd been following me. I dismissed it as imagination but . . ."

She gave him the patient look she had perfected in her teaching days. It said she expected an answer to a question she hadn't even asked. She was willing to wait a long time for that answer, provided it was the one she considered appropriate.

"Okay, I'll hand it over then. God knows what I'll say. 'Sorry Max, but I happened to notice this syringe that just attached itself to my shoe,' or—"

"Just tell him it slipped your mind. . . ." Tenderly, she kissed the bald part of his head. "As things tend to do these days."

■ "Dad! Holy shit! Dad, come here!"

"Jake! What's wrong?" Jim came running. He looked relieved to find Jake whole as he entered his room. "From the language you're using I thought you'd been shot!"

"Yeah, sorry about that but . . . this is massive, Dad. Unbelievable."

"What *are* you talking about!"

"The screen. Read the screen. It's the code on the disk I found and like it had this code in crazy letters and numbers and the keyboard guy talked about music codes on the afternoon rock show and—"

"Slow down. Let me take a look at what's so—" The display on the screen stopped Jim dead in his tracks. "Holy shit!"

"Yeah, that's what I said."

"I can see why. If this is what it looks like, someone's running drugs."

"And whoever it is uses the school computers!" Jake was excited.

"And you seem to have intercepted their records. I wouldn't be so excited about all this, because if it's true, Jake, this is playing with dynamite."

"What do you mean, *if* it's true? It's got to be true."

"I sure as hell hope not. Where did this information come from anyway?"

"This'll take a few minutes, Dad, and it sounds like sci-fi, but—"

"Slow down, slow down. How 'bout starting at the beginning, okay?"

"Okay. Well, remember I told you about the fire yesterday."

"Uh-huh."

"Well, after the fire department shoved off, I went in to get my disks off the computer . . ."

As Jake talked, the look on Jim's face alternated between incredulity and grave concern, as the implications expanded in his mind. After Jake had told him everything he could recall, Jim sat with his head in his hands for several minutes. Finally he spoke. His voice was very quiet.

"We have to wonder, first of all, if this is just a hoax of some sort."

"But why the code?"

"That's true, people who perpetrate hoaxes wouldn't likely make it this difficult to crack a code. Unless someone happened to be a musician—"

"Or tune in to the right TV show like I did today?"

"That's right. And if someone really did get into the room, and even, well, say they did knock you out, there's no real sign of that, is there?"

"But everything on the hard drive was erased, Dad." He saw how hard it was for Jim to come to grips with the situation. It was so improbable. "And I know what you're thinking. You think I'm imagining stuff, like she always did. But I'm really not.

Honest. Like I said, everything on the hard drive was erased when I got up this morning."

"It's been known to happen before—some electrical disturbance, or say you're like sleepwalking or, I don't know . . ." He shook his head, clearly unwilling to believe the dreadful possibility facing them both. "You're sure this is the original? And the copy you made is gone? Absolutely?"

"Grandma cleaned the room."

"That settles it. If it were in the wrong place, she'd have found it! But wait a minute. Maybe it's slipped under the computer or behind the workstation or—"

"Well, I haven't actually checked around there." Jake sounded deflated.

"Look, son, I do trust you absolutely, but let's check. Because before we do anything we have to be sure. Dead sure."

"Guess so."

Jim looked under the raiser that held the Power Mac at the angle Jake preferred. A space big enough for stray pencils, pocket calculators, and disks to hide—as he'd found in the past. "No, nothing under it. Nothing between the monitor and the works."

Maybe Jake was wrong. "Let's wheel the whole thing out and check behind the desk then." The unit rolled smoothly from the wall on its oversize casters. As he pulled it away from the wall, he saw his father's eyes widen. "Dad, what's wrong?"

Jim's voice sounded husky as he yanked a small plastic box from the back of the computer. "Just this. Someone had a wireless transducer attached to this computer. Everything you've been loading or typing or playing has been transmitted to a receiver somewhere!"

"Yes!" Jake slammed the air above his head with his fist.

"You out of your mind?"

"It just proves what I told you—and Joyce the Voice. Wait'll she hears this—she said it was just my imagination, lack of sleep and all that." He reached for the phone.

"Wait. Let's just keep everyone out of this for now—until we're sure of what we're actually dealing with, anyway."

"What should we do now?"

"Get a printout of everything you've decoded. While you're doing it, I'm going to trade this drink in on a strong black coffee. Want me to bring you a Pepsi?" Jake nodded as Jim left the room, only to return immediately. He went to the window, looked around, and then drew the curtain.

"Why'd you do that?"

"I want to make sure the window's secure, that's all. Be right back."

Jake pushed control P, and the printer whined into action. Its relentless printout of pure trouble had begun.

■ "Someone waiting to see you, Chief," the officer on the desk said. "Egghead from the school. Says your wife told him he could find you here."

"I've told her time and again never to tell anyone

where I—oh, it's okay. Family friend." He recognized the visitor outside his office. "Martin," he called jovially, "what brings you here at this hour?"

"Maybe the same thing that keeps you here at this hour. Couldn't help overhearing conversations about our garbage compactor and your investigation."

"They're wonderful, these boys. Always gossiping."

"Look, Chief, there's something been troubling me."

"Come into the office. You want a beer?"

"Didn't think you were allowed to drink on duty."

"I reckon this is my own time—after eight on a Saturday night for God's sake. Anyway, this fridge is off-limits—I got the only key. I smuggle my cans in full, take 'em out empty. In my gym bag. Now, you want one or not?"

"Unless you've got something stronger, I'd love a beer, thanks. Look, Max, there's something I have to tell you right away. It's something I should have told you before."

Max popped the top of a beer can and handed it across. "Wouldn't happen to be about a hypodermic needle you hid with your shoe yesterday, would it?"

"I should have known better than to try it with you. I thought if it ever got out it'd make the school look bad. After all, we just got over that incident with the previous janitor."

"Well, here we go again. Because that needle you hid contained pure heroin with a little something extra we haven't quite figured out yet. But the lab's working on it—overtime."

"How can you possibly know that? Did you find some fluid on the ground?"

"Course not—it was in the hypodermic barrel. You look weird, Martin."

Martin reached into his pocket and handed the chief an envelope. "This is the one I covered up with my shoe. I slipped it in my pocket and—"

The chief's eyes had that icy look. "You know how stupid that makes you? Concealing something is one thing, but taking evidence away—really, Martin."

"I know. Sorry."

The two men sat in silence. Finally Max took a slug of his beer and opened the top drawer on his beat-up oak desk. He showed Martin the plastic bag and tapped its contents. "This is the needle we found in the compactor. What's more, we got prints off it. Against all odds, the Prof actually got us a thumbprint. It's already gone to Interpol—prints don't match any of ours. Of course, it may be someone local who's never been in trouble before."

"Oh God." Martin buried his head in his hands. "I feel like Anne's right."

"What's Anne being right about now?"

"She had a feeling—call it a premonition—that something really terrible is happening all around us. Something that goes back to Jeremy Carson and those marks on his neck."

"That wife of yours is pretty smart."

"You mean she's right?"

The chief looked at him for a few seconds, took a deep breath, and unlocked the file drawer in his desk. "I think it's time to fill you in on something so strange and so terrible that you won't want to believe it. What I've got to tell you is something I wasn't going to. Because when I knew you'd hidden something, I started to have my suspicions—started wondering about you, even." He thought Martin looked hurt but continued. "Then I realized you could never be a very good criminal Martin. You said you were tying your shoe and you were wearing loafers. You look like a kid who's just been caught telling a whopper!" He chuckled.

Martin attempted to compose himself. He *did* feel like a kid who'd been caught. But that was only part of it. He knew there was worse to come.

"Anyhow, this thing just gets worse. And Anne has hit the nail right on the head. Because back when Jeremy Carson died, we had word from the top that there could be a link between their toy company and drugs. After he 'had his heart attack in the bath,' the trail went suddenly cold. As if someone nearby got scared and backed off."

"The marks on his neck?"

"The people at the top—and this was international by now—wanted to keep that quiet. Theory was, maybe there was no connection with the people we were after. It was investigated on the side, and very thoroughly too. But it still didn't add up."

"And our previous janitor?"

"I wonder if there's a connection. I wonder if he

saw something he wasn't meant to see? Well, it's a theory. But the thing that came from the cops in Japan was the part you won't like. They think someone's been tapping into your computer system and using it to help them operate an international drug racket."

"I don't see how our system could—"

"The drug *business* is just that—it's run just like any international business. Needs communication. Shipping schedules. Records of payment. Your system is wide open for a good twelve, maybe fifteen hours a day. Given the time difference, it could be mighty useful. What we really need now is some kind of proof that it has been—or is being—used by outsiders. That'd tell us if all these theories are right or not."

"What kind of proof could there be?"

"Like I said, proof that the system has been used by strangers."

"It's almost impossible to pinpoint the way it's used. We access everything—here and overseas. We've got the best information network of any institution in the country. We can communicate with everything. Bulletin boards, libraries, airlines, you name it. And what's more, we can access countries from Brazil to the UK without any problem."

"All thanks to old Jeremy Carson."

"That's right. But I don't see how *that* can possibly be connected. We didn't get the system until after he died."

"Mmm. That's true enough. Probably a coincidence, but the possibility of any connection of any kind has got to be followed through."

Martin felt sick to his stomach. "Don't know if this is relevant or not, but there was a yellow car nearly ran me down just after the fire—"

"That old gossip Lila Spooner—the one with the dog. *She* mentioned a yellow car as well." The chief was thoughtful. "Maybe the old bat has taken to adding real facts to her stories. If she is—" His train of thought was interrupted by the telephone. "Pink here. Yeah operator, I'll hold. . . . Yes it is . . . yeah . . . this afternoon . . . just around eight P.M. our time . . . Yeah?" He scribbled furiously as he listened. "But this is unbelievable! . . . What? . . . Oh my God . . . Yes sir, I certainly will. And look, I better give you my private number at home, it's unlisted." He gave the caller his number, said goodbye, and slowly replaced the receiver in its cradle. He looked at Martin, paused, and then spoke. "I guess you better know this, Martin. Because it concerns you in a way you're not going to like one little bit. Those prints we found on the hypodermic from your school—they belong to a Nazi war criminal!"

"And he's still loose? After all these *years*?"

"Apparently Interpol lost track of him in the forties."

"But what could he possibly have been doing at our school?"

"That, my friend, is something we had better find out. But *fast*. Apparently he was a doctor. Involved in mind experiments. Not only does this psycho like screwing up people's brains, he actually *enjoys* watching them die."

■As his Mercedes sped toward the tin mine Jan Mulder watched neat lines of yellow flame licking the twilight sky. How different things were since he'd first seen the Cairns cane fields in 1944. Back then, they used to "burn off" much less frequently, and the harvest was more or less an annual affair. But these days, the harvesting period seemed to last forever. When Jan arrived in Australia, the war had fueled a seemingly endless demand for the sugar crop. Today, however, times were tough. International competition made cane farming a dicey vocation. Much of the land had been subdivided for project housing when the market had worsened. But this week, there would still be many fires in the area. When dusk approached and the winds receded, the underbrush would yield to the purifying flames that cleared the way for the harvesting machines. The charred cane would be cut and placed on miniature trains that ran the narrow gauge rails to central collection points. From there, they journeyed to the sugar refineries for crushing. The cane's juices would wind up sweetening everything from cakes to colas, the fibrous remains processed into dozens of useful by-products, from fiberboard to fuel.

The stretch limo slowed as the uniformed chauffeur guided it into the private roadway known only to Jan's inner circle. Just half an hour from home, Jan thought how much he loved these warm spring evenings, the way they suddenly turned into the hot tropical summers he had dreamed of during that bitter winter in Auschwitz. He stretched out in the back of the limousine, and for the first time in weeks allowed himself to relax. And reminisce.

chapter seven

Sydney, 1960

"Jan Mulder! You don't look a day older!" Jeremy shook Jan's hand vigorously.

"Ah, but I must. It *has* been thirteen years."

"So it has. If it weren't for Christmas cards, we'd really be out of touch. How are things?"

"Fairly good. But so much competition these days I've decided to diversify. I'm also working on computer-based ideas now."

"What about toys? When are you going to come up with the big idea for us to manufacture? For a very good deal, of course, *old boy*."

Jan laughed. "I remember that discussion well. It's partly why I'm in Sydney, to tell you about my progress in that direction. I think I'm on to one of the biggest ideas ever!"

"I'm all ears," Jeremy said.

"Remember we talked about television and toys. Putting them together. Well, I think we have to add something else to that. The computer. If we could put a small computer in a box and have it move things around on a TV screen—controlled by a player, of course—we would have the ultimate toy. A color television game."

"Mmm. And people would go to an exhibit to play these games?"

"No, no. They'd be in ordinary homes. Can you imagine the market?"

"Now this *is* fantasyland. A computer is as big as a lounge room, at least the IBM 704 is. And even if you had one of those, how could you move things around on a screen?"

"I believe I can. I'm on the verge of perfecting a raster system. And please don't ask me to explain it unless you have a year. But believe me, Jeremy, with my raster system, an ordinary TV set, and a small computer, there is a future."

Jeremy was unconvinced. "Surely this is a long way away."

"I don't believe so. There is work being done already at MIT. They're being very secretive, but things are beginning to happen."

"Well, soon as you get closer, let me know. Now, let's go and have that lunch. If you've got a few minutes later on, Joyce is dying to see you again. And we can't wait to show off our son, Jim."

"How old is he now?"

"Thirteen." Jeremy beamed. "He's a math wizard —absolutely fascinated by computers too. And talk about a natural football talent . . ."

■The Mercedes pulled to a stop, and the sound of the corrugated iron wall sliding into the ground brought Jan back from his reminiscing. Such a shame, Jeremy Carson. They could all have been such friends. Jeremy, his son Jim, and now his grandson Jake. If only they hadn't tried to cheat him, ridicule him. He picked up the intercom and spoke to the chauffeur. "Horst, call Werner. Tell him to prepare something *extraspecial* for me."

"Right away. Feeling better for your nap, sir?"

"Much. Thank you, Horst." He smiled as the elevator lowered the Mercedes down the concrete shaft into the bunker. Outside, the iron wall returned to its normal position. To an outsider it simply looked like another abandoned shed at the edge of a cane field.

■ "How many pages did you get?" Jim asked as the printer head parked itself in standby position.

"Let's see—forty-nine. And there's all kinds of weird stuff on it," Jake answered. "Most of it doesn't make much sense, though."

"I'm sure it will to someone. Right now, we better tell Chief Pink what's been happening. Give me the phone."

He dialed Max's home number and got his wife. "Hi Jeannie, sorry to call you at this hour, but I need to speak to Max kind of urgently. . . . I see . . . how soon do you think that'll be? Do you have a direct number, I don't want to let anyone else know what it's about . . . yeah, it really is that important. . . . I understand. Well, can you get a message through to him? Thanks a lot."

"What's happening?"

"She doesn't want to give out his direct number, but she'll call him right away."

As they waited, the pair tried to make sense of the printout. A lot of it seemed to be shipping details. There were lists and weights of various drugs, financial records, and what appeared to be some kind of diary. The dates went back to 1941. A lot of the information was obviously in German. Jim recognized place names like Berlin and Auschwitz, but the sentences connecting them were a mystery. Other countries were listed, but some—especially Argentina—appeared over and over again. When the phone rang they both jumped.

"Hello, Jim Carson here . . . Max, this is a long story but . . . sorry, I can't come in tomorrow but—it's basically about a computer disk Jake found by accident at the school. It was a code, and he's cracked it . . . no, it's not a game. Unless you call shipping schedules for drugs—yeah, that's what I thought. You want us to come down and see you or . . . just me and Jake . . . no, we haven't told anyone . . . okay, we'll stay put." There was a long pause. "Now you're scaring me, Max . . . I guarantee we'll be careful." He hung up and turned to Jake. "Son, you've found something that is so dangerous it can't be overstated. Max wants us to be extremely quiet about this until things are under control. We're not to talk to anyone about it. In other words, total silence on the entire subject. And we're to be very careful *personally* for the next little while. Hey, what are you doing?"

"Oh, just making another copy of the disk—you never know when they'll knock you out and steal your stuff!" Jake was trying to make light of things, but underneath the forced humor he was scared. *Really* scared.

Max arrived in his own car and out of uniform. "Don't know if I'd fool anyone, but it's the best I can do at the moment. Lee will be joining us in a few minutes. I told him to ditch the uniform for this meeting. Anyway, I hope you're not too tired, Jake, this could go on for a while."

"I'm okay, Chief. You think we're really in danger?"

"If whoever's behind this thinks you're the only one with their disk, you might be. But if they think lots of people have copies, there's no reason for them to bother with you. No reason at all."

"What if they want revenge?"

"Only if it's a loner—a psycho. And I think this is a big operation. So you can rule that out. Still, you have to be careful, specially for the next few days or so." There was a gentle knocking at the door. "That's something you may never hear again, boys. One of my cops doing a subtle door knock." The cold eyes again belied the smile, but they appreciated that Max was trying to lessen the tension as he opened the door for the young officer. "You know Lee?" he asked. Jake nodded; Jim and the young cop shook hands. The chief started asking questions, and Lee made notes in shorthand.

An hour later, Max folded up the printout and

carefully put it down on the coffee table. He turned to Lee: "What do you think?"

The young cop thought for a while. "I think the first thing is to ensure the safety of everyone in this house."

"Good," Max agreed. "Anything else?"

"We need a German translator we can trust." Lee was thinking out loud. "The translation programs at the school are probably a bit too literal."

"What the hell do you mean?" Max muttered.

"Just that they translate word for word, so if there are subtleties in the language, you'd miss out on them. The program is really just a German-English dictionary."

"Surely it'd give us a pretty good idea of what's in this—I don't want a whole lot of people involved. Not that what I want has much to do with things. I've been told from the highest international authorities to keep this as quiet as we can."

"In that case, let's run the direct translation. How do we set it up?"

"Talk to Martin Oliver—he's aware of this." He caught Lee's disapproving glance. "He's involved as he can be, don't worry."

"What if he's actually Mr. Big?" Jake asked.

Max laughed. "Martin's a good principal but he couldn't fix a bingo game. No, whoever's at the top of this thing does a lot of traveling, a lot of administration. And you may find Mr. Big, as you call him, is actually a group of people heading a huge organization. One with all kinds of employees all over the world."

"From what I can see in that printout, the chief's right," Lee told Jake.

"I better cancel my trip to Cairns tomorrow," Jim said.

"I don't think you should start changing plans."

"I'm not leaving Jake alone here, not after what happened to him last night."

"He won't be alone. This house will be under total surveillance about ten minutes from now. Lee here is liaising with the Commonwealth Police bodyguards."

"I'll double-check their arrival time now. You got a phone I can use in private?"

Jim gestured. "Down the hall. Look, Max, I still don't like the idea of being away. Even if it is just for the day."

"Just the day? Then you *really* shouldn't worry. In fact, I have a feeling that whoever's behind all this knows damn well the code is wide open now."

"Can you tell where the bug came from?"

"I can't, Jake. Maybe someone in the lab. But I doubt it. It's made in Germany, probably one of thousands."

"What if it didn't work? What if they don't know the code is cracked?"

The chief thought. "Then there may still be danger. But it's not likely. People have gone to a lot of bother to bug your system." He spoke to Jake with total conviction. "I think, for you, the problem is over. For us? It's probably just beginning. But I can promise you this—you *will* be safe here."

"I'll confirm that," Lee said as he rejoined the

group. "You've got two top men. One of them even keeps an eye on the queen when she visits. Good enough for you guys?"

Jake looked happy; Jim was still unsure. "Well, you should be," Max said in a that's-all-for-now voice. He suddenly looked mischievous. "Now, we can go and get Martin Oliver to open up and run this translation. No sleep for him tonight. Serves him right too. Lee, any word on that thumbprint yet?"

"They're still working on it. What they'd like right away is Jake's printout—they need to digi-fax a copy to Interpol. Want me to drop it off?"

"Better if you stay here till the guards arrive. I'll give them a copy and take the disk to the school." He turned to Jake. "They can get a paper copy out of this disk at your school?"

"Sure—it's the same basic program—mine can do a few more things, that's all."

"Yes," Max scolded. "Like getting into the town council computer files."

"I was only fourteen then."

"Huh! Oh, Lee, you can have the fun of picking Martin Oliver up and dragging him to his office at this ungodly hour. If you're really unlucky you might meet his wife." Lee raised his eyebrows in question. "Smart as hell but if you step out of line with her . . ." He made a gesture of cutting his throat.

Lee shook his head in resignation as the chief left the room with Jim.

"Totally out of touch," Jake volunteered.

"Totally," Lee echoed. "Hey. My kid brother says you've got a room full of swim trophies—how about showing me while we wait for the feds?"

"That's cool." They went to Jake's room as Jim saw Max out the door.

"You sure about this, Max?"

"He'll be totally safe. This thing involves drugs on a big scale. And that usually means secrecy is just a joke. The minute that fax hits the wire the world'll know. Jake'll be no threat because he'll have no secrets. The people running this operation won't waste their time on revenge—except among their own. No, they'll be too busy regrouping. The shipping schedules will pinpoint a few loads, but those shipments won't even be claimed from the wharves. They'll likely just write them off, we'll get a few little guys, and the world will keep on spinning. Just like it always does."

"I like it better when you're folksy. Tonight you're too cynical."

"I'm a realist tonight, Jim. And the realist still has one nagging concern about you and your family. I can't help wondering if there was ever a connection between your late father and the drug business."

"We both know he did a lot of terrible things in business, but I can't imagine drugs in the mix."

"Neither can I. But there's still that puzzle."

"The marks on his neck?"

"Like the marks on the original school janitor's neck when he OD'd."

"Did he *really* OD?"

"Did your father *really* have a heart attack? And the bigger question for me will always be your breakdown at that meeting. I still believe you were drugged. Still believe someone did it to destroy the family company."

"I'd almost be grateful if it were true. Then I could get on with my life knowing I am sane and that it won't happen again. At other times, I dunno. That could mean someone's got a grudge against us. Someone who's still a danger. Maybe I'm better off not knowing any more than I do now."

"Maybe so. Anyhow, try and have a good trip up to Cairns. If you need me, just call. Here's my private number." He gave Jim a card.

"I appreciate that. Oh—and I promise *not* to give it to Lila Spooner."

The chief patted Jim on the back and they parted smiling.

chapter eight

In the bunker beneath the tin mine, Jan placed his thumb on the laserscan lock, and the door to his elegant private quarters glided open. He crossed the room filled with priceless antiques and sat on the comfortable overstuffed leather sofa. He clicked a button, and a padded footrest swung into place. He keyed a remote control to activate the DAT and soon the opening bars of Wagner's *Götterdämmerung* flooded the huge soundproofed room. Shortly, a flashing light on a control panel built into the granite coffee table caught his attention. He flicked a switch, and across the room an original Rembrandt slid from its frame to reveal a massive TV monitor. He recognized Werner and smiled. He touched a thumbprint laserscan on the table, and its minicomputer accepted the match. The door glided open and Werner entered. Eighteen years old, he dressed the same as the other young guards—black leather jeans, Doc Martens, and a black tank top. And, like the rest, the young neo-Nazi was a skinhead. He crossed the plush pile maroon carpet to place a small silver tray beside the Rodin sculpture on the table. He removed a black linen napkin covering a loaded syringe and a tourniquet.

"Horst said you wanted something special tonight."

"Very good, Werner, what have we this time?"

"Enhanced heroin. Ninety percent pure with a mild hallucinogenic, plus a few little extras. Nothing too tiring. I understand you want to work a couple of hours later."

"Yes, I want to finalize some important preparations for a guest or two."

"Guests?" Werner's pale blue eyes sparkled.

"Our famous contestant will soon play the final part of the game. The ultimate event in our new sensudrome."

"How soon?"

"Anxious!"

"We've all been waiting so long for it that—"

"I understand your enthusiasm, but after all, you've only been waiting ten years. For me, the culmination of a lifetime's work will soon be a reality. The moment of truth, you might say. Now, come back in two hours with something for wakefulness, and how about some lobster or prawns or—what do you suggest?"

"Barramundi, from one of the company's own boats beyond the reef."

"That sounds wonderful. Fillet and sauté it. With shredded almonds and lemon, I think."

"And wine?"

"Tonight," he said, tightening the tourniquet above his elbow, "I feel like a Moët. A precelebration celebration, you might say."

"Very good." Werner clicked his heels and bowed. He marched proudly from the room, his silver swastika earring flashing as he passed the light focused on the original Gauguin—a priceless oil painting the Nazis took from the Louvre in 1942. The door opened briefly for his exit.

With absolute precision, Jan slid the needle into the center of his vein and emptied the contents of the syringe into his bloodstream. He unfastened the tourniquet, turned up the volume, and proceeded to sink into a cocoon of soft leather upholstery, Wagner, and drug-induced contentment.

■The federal bodyguards had arrived, and Lee went to collect Martin Oliver. As Jim packed his briefcase for the trip to Cairns, he talked with Jake in a way he never had before. "I don't quite know why I feel I ought to delve into the family secrets, but I always knew they would come up sooner or later. Better you hear it from me, I guess. The way things are shaping up, you're liable to get a sordid media account of our family any minute."

"This sounds heavy."

"Too heavy for you to handle when you were younger. Anyway, I'll keep it as short as I can. It started the night your grandparents were married. They met a Dutchman on the flight to London."

"On their honeymoon . . ."

"Right. A dark horse, Mother always said. Anyway, he was an inventor who loved music and mind games. Years later, he came to Dad and told him he'd found out how to put tones and moving objects on a silicone chip. He claimed to be the first person to do that."

"Was he? I thought it all started in Silicone Valley."

"Not according to the Dutchman. What is true is that he brought this apparatus to Father in the form of the first true home video game anyone at the toy company had ever seen."

"Doomkritters."

"That's right. But when he brought the electronics to Dad, all he wanted him to do was design the chassis and joysticks. Apparently Dad agreed to share the profits with him. Dad organized the joysticks and the chassis—the design and the molds. But at the same time, according to the Dutchman, Dad stole his idea for the electronics, then allegedly sold the entire package to the Japanese, but he kept royalties for our company."

"Is it true? Grandma always says Granddad invented Doomkritters all by himself."

"She doesn't want to think anything bad about him. But I have a feeling she says 'all by himself' too often."

"Like she's trying to convince us?"

"Trying to convince herself is more like it. Anyway, the Dutchman tried to sue Dad, and there was a court case. And it was pretty nasty. Dad's lawyer made the Dutchman look like a fool."

"I thought you said he was brilliant."

"He was. It's just that in those days Australia had a biased mentality. You could have a Ph.D. where you came from, but if you spoke with an accent, they treated you like a moron."

"That still happens at our school."

"Not to the same extent, I hope. Anyway, the Dutchman snapped—left the court screaming that he'd ultimately destroy the entire Carson family. Dad said he was actually frothing at the mouth when they dragged him away."

"Sounds like *Night of the Samurai Werewolf*."

"It was no movie. He used to phone and threaten all kinds of things—until they put a restraining order on him. Finally he sold his share of his business and went back home to Europe."

"What happened then?"

"He was never heard of again."

"Do you think this is connected with Granddad's death?"

"It's possible. It could even be related to the way he died. If you believe the chief, it might even be about why he died."

"But Granddad had a heart attack in his bathtub and drowned—the night the stock market crashed."

"That is the official story."

"You mean it isn't true?"

"We hope it *is* true. Not that a heart attack is a wonderful thing. It's just that if there was foul play involved, it could mean a killer is still on the loose. I think Max believes that's the case."

"Did he say so?"

"Look, Jake. You better know this. Something

unexplainable. When your granddad died, they found some strange marks on his neck."

"Marks? Like what kind of marks?"

"As if—and this is so crazy—as if he'd been bitten by a crocodile."

"In the bathtub?"

"Told you it was bizarre. Then the same thing happened again. Four months ago. When Mr. Hoskin—"

"The janitor before Old Redders?"

"Yes. Hoskin apparently OD'd on heroin. Again, in his bathtub. And they found the same marks on *his* body. Max figures it's connected with drugs. Maybe the old janitor saw something he shouldn't have."

"Well, someone was using the school computers to relay information somewhere. Maybe he did see something. But Granddad? I don't get it."

"I'm sure not . . . But why those crocodile marks on their bodies?"

"The only crocodile I ever saw in a living room is the one in our Doomkritters game." As he said the words, his speech slowed and his eyes widened. "Dad! The crocodile in Doomkritters grabs the loser by the neck and drowns him."

"Oh my God! Suppose the Dutchman was around when my father died. And suppose he's back to make good his threat of revenge!"

"If he is, it's like he's playing Doomkritters for real. The croc marks, the drownings—they're like a calling card."

"Wait a minute. Let's think this through. He

promised revenge, revenge on the family. Thank God you weren't born then, so—"

"So it was Granddad and you he threatened— Dad, you gotta be careful—supercareful."

"I think I better talk to the chief right away." Jim grabbed the phone and the card Max had given him with his mobile number. He got through immediately. "Max, it's Jim Carson. I think Jake has just figured out the connection between the deaths of my father and the previous school janitor!"

■Werner injected Jan Mulder with fifteen milliliters of buffered Naloxone. The effect was immediate. "Thank you, Werner, that was all very pleasant."

"A bit sooner than you requested, sir. Dr. Engells wanted to see you before he returns to Argentina, and I thought perhaps before your dinner?"

"Fine. Show him in."

The doctor set up his laptop computer at one end of the nine-foot-long marble table Jan usually reserved for dining. "I have your computer-enhanced sketches for discussion. I want to have the implants tooled, so perhaps we can finalize a few remaining details."

"Excellent, but I hate staring at those tiny screens. Werner, patch this through to the projection unit."

The Rembrandt slid from its position. A six-by-nine-foot picture of Jan filled the screen.

"This is as you are today. Now, if we alter the chin line with a silicone implant like so . . ." He keyed some instructions to his computer, and the rather pointed chin became broad. "Yes?"

"Chin looks a bit bizarre, don't you feel?"

"How about this, then?" Using the mouse, he contoured the chin line slightly. "Of course, all the loose flesh in the neck is cut away too. . . ."

"Yes, that's better."

"Two cheekbone implants like this." He entered a few more keystrokes, and the cheekbones became more prominent. "While we're at it, you might as well lose the bump in your nose, so the rhinoplasty I propose does this." The nose became classic. "And there's a lot of loose flesh around the eyes. The upper lids can be modified as well, giving us this." The picture became that of a much younger man.

"It looks fine, except—the eyebrows seem strange, somehow."

"They are. Until we remove a one-inch strip of skin and hair from the top of your head, which raises the eyebrows like so. As you can see, the hairline does recede slightly. But if it concerns you, a transplant can be arranged. Finally . . ." He entered some figures. "I thought a change of hairstyle and color . . . some brown-colored contact lenses and . . ."

"Brilliant! I hope I can live up to this youthful new face!"

The doctor was without humor and failed to recognize the tiny joke. "We can do nothing about that. What happens after the surgery must always be the patient's responsibility."

"Fingerprints?"

"A donor has been located."

"An anonymous donor, I trust?"

The surgeon was irritated by the question. "Obviously the donor has been selected carefully. You will receive the fingerprints of someone who has never undergone any identification procedure—the person chosen has never had a passport, driver's license, identity card—nothing. Not only is he anonymous, he is totally unaware of what is about to occur. Now, about my fee."

"Seven hundred thousand U.S. dollars were placed in your Swiss account yesterday."

"Very good. I will, of course, have that verified before we proceed. I look forward to meeting you in Buenos Aires. And, Doctor . . ."

"Yes, Doctor?"

"The last surgeon to alter your appearance died soon after the surgery. Should that happen to me, the same will happen to you." He snapped his briefcase shut. "Now I must hurry to Sydney. The prime minister's wife is tiring of the message in her mirror." He walked briskly from the room.

chapter nine

"I nearly got myself shot walking up your driveway just now. Those federal bodyguards are cowboys!"

"Glad to hear they're alert," Jim said as he showed Max Pink and Martin Oliver inside.

"Brought Martin along to talk to Jake. Then maybe we can all get some sleep. Martin's getting a German translator to see if there are any subtleties in this printout. And I got a copy for you as well. Perhaps there's some reference that may trigger something we can use. We'll get you a new copy when the final translation's done. Now, when will that be, Martin?"

"Getting someone on Sunday won't be easy. But I have a couple of people in mind. I'm sure by three o'clock tomorrow afternoon, though—"

"Excellent. Now, how about you talk to Jake about your other problem while Martin fills me in on *his* problem."

"Yes. Jake, mind if we sit down?"

"'S cool. Uh, sir." Jake couldn't understand why Egghead Oliver was being so polite to him. "What's happening?"

"I think, first of all, we have to thank you for your part in this. Breaking that code could not have been easy. And I hope you use this talent you have for constructive purposes."

"Martin." Max was testy. "If you're going to turn this into a teacher-student speech, we'll be here all night. Jim, can we go somewhere else and talk?"

"Yeah. Come into the next room. You want a coffee or a beer?"

They left Martin and Jake alone.

"Everybody's irritable and far too easily upset," Martin told Jake. "I suppose we're just not used to dealing with anything like this. And on top of everything else, I have a young man—about your age—arriving tomorrow. His name is Tony Orsini. From L.A. His father is coming out to do a research project for the government in a month, and they thought rather than have Tony start another semester there, he might as well settle in here. He's a bit like you—very bright in computer science, and a fine boy. I've met him a few times."

Jake was afraid Egghead Oliver was starting to ramble again. "So what's the story, sir?"

"Ah, yes. I have to pick the boy up at the airport around six A.M., but then I have to spend a lot of time organizing this translation thing for Max, uh, the chief of police."

"I know who Max is."

Martin ignored Jake's interjection. "Well, your

father, I understand, is going out of town on business for the day. So you'll be on your own."

"Don't forget the bodyguards outside."

"Yes, of course. In any case, I'd really appreciate it if you could spend the day with Tony. Show him around a bit." He offered the ultimate carrot. "If you like, I'll give you the keys to the computer lab. I intended to show it to him myself, but circumstances and all."

Jake welcomed the idea. Though he was basically a loner, this was one time he looked forward to having company around. "I guess I could handle it, sir."

Martin was relieved. "I can bring him here straight from the airport. Alternatively, I could take him home and leave him with my wife, and you could all meet later."

Jake figured jet lag and the principal's wife were a heavy combination for a new kid to handle. "You can bring him right here from the airport, we got heaps of stuff for breakfast."

"If you're sure that's convenient."

"I'm sure. Dad leaves for the airport around seven anyway. Hey, this guy—Tony—do you think he'd like to go swimming?"

"I'd imagine so—he certainly looks athletic enough. But now you can tell me something while we're waiting for Max and your father. How on earth did you break this code? How did you even know where to begin? Did you use any of the logic programs we teach, or . . ."

For the first time since they met eight years ago,

Jake held the principal spellbound as he retraced the events involved in unraveling the cipher.

In the next room, Max and Jim were still discussing Jake's latest discovery.

"This Doomkritters crocodile," Max was saying, "it's the final part of the game?"

"Yeah. There's a little guy on the screen. He represents you, the player. You have to steer your way through this jungle. There are all kinds of things you have to do. Jump over quicksand, avoid the platinum lions, the barbed-wire gorillas. All kinds of hazards. You get a hundred points every time you bump one of them off. If you just avoid them, you get fifty points. But if the stainless steel crocodile gets you at the end, he snaps his jaws around your throat and drags you under the water. The game gives you thirty seconds before you run out of breath. If you can zap him in that time, you win. But it's the tricky part of the game. If you fire into water, things deflect."

"Like in real life," Max observed.

"I guess. Anyhow, hitting the crocodile is part luck, part skill."

"Sounds just like the police force. But, let's say it was the Dutchman that killed your father and now, years later, the last janitor. What was he doing in the meantime? So many things still left up in the air. For instance—" His mobile phone cut across the conversation. "Max Pink. At the Carsons' place, Lee. Hang on, get my notebook. Okay, shoot. Uh-huh . . . uh-huh . . . oh brother! Yeah, see you soon."

He pushed the disconnect button on his telephone and turned to Jim. "This is beyond belief. The prints on the hypo from the school? We knew it was a Nazi war criminal. Now we know who it was. A Doktor Johannes Wasser. Neurosurgeon. Mind experiments. Here's the connection. This Nazi went to Holland during the war, then came to Australia. Only he changed his name. To Jan Mulder. The man who claimed he really invented Doomkritters."

Jim sat down slowly, trying to take all this information in. "Then he's still around. But where is he hiding?" Jake and Martin came into the room looking concerned.

"Heard shouting, I thought."

"I was getting excited and loud. Bad habit." Max explained, "We just found out that Jim's father's archenemy left his fingerprints on the hypodermic we found at your school."

"I thought he disappeared just after the stock market crashed," Martin said.

"Well, he's back. What's more, he used to be a Nazi neurosurgeon who performed some of the cruelest experiments of the war. His real name was Doktor Johannes Wasser. Changed his fingerprints and his name—came out here as Jan Mulder. Interpol's only just made the connection."

Jim noticed Jake was deep in concentration and muttering to himself. "You okay, son? I guess it's pretty late and—"

Jake held his hand up for quiet. "Just . . . a . . . sec. Our new janitor—Old Redders."

Martin reverted to principal mode: "You mean our new janitor Mr. Redlum."

"Yeah," Jake said. "That's it."

"What are you getting at son?" Max asked.

"Redlum. It's an anagram. Spell Redlum backwards and you get M-U-L-D-E-R."

"Jan Mulder! He's been under our very noses—posing as a janitor," Jim said.

"So damned sure of himself he plays games with his name!" Martin shook his head in amazement.

"Must be a bit psycho. The other thing we got on him is this: he's not only a vicious killer—he's a real hardened junkie!"

Martin Oliver sighed. "How the plot thickens."

"It's going to get a lot thicker," Max said. "We'll send someone around to pick him up—although it's a waste of time."

"Why?" Jake asked.

"Because this man is smart—if he knows we're on to him, he's smart enough to change his fingerprints, smart enough to change his identity. This is one guy that's a *real* survivor. If you hadn't cracked that code, he'd still be around us—still be a real threat. No, I guess he'll be long gone by now—probably right out of the country. And I just hope to hell I'm right."

"Amen," said Jim.

Jake decided he'd better set the alarm. It was almost midnight, and he wanted to be up at six to see his dad before he left for Cairns. The news of Old Redders and Jan Mulder being one and the same was awesome. To think he'd also been a Nazi war criminal was really frightening—especially since the danger had been so close to home. But tonight the bodyguards were near, and the chief was probably right—Mulder was far from Sydney by now. So much had happened in the past twenty-four hours. Well, at least tonight everyone could sleep peacefully.

As he lay in bed going over the events of the past day and a half, Jake was still attempting to understand the way he felt about his life, and especially his parents. Things had changed so much since his mother, Jasmine, had left home.

At first he felt alone and, in a way, betrayed. Then he realized that, day to day, things were much the same as they'd always been. He missed Jasmine, yet his grandmother seemed to make things run more smoothly than they had when his mother was around. His dad seemed less tense, and for the first time they had wonderful conversations. Conversations that had never been possible before. When his mother was around, she seemed determined to interrupt any communication she was not included in. Even now, Jake still felt guilty for even having these thoughts. *After all, you're supposed to love your mother, aren't you?*

But increasingly, he couldn't help feeling relieved that she'd gone away. Especially at school functions where the parents and the teaching staff got together. There the other mothers seemed so casual and natural about their children's accomplishments. Jasmine was always a little louder, always seemed to demand a little more attention than the others. He could feel the impatience turn to polite resignation when she insisted on making one of her impromptu "speeches" at PTA meetings. He was proud of the way she was more glamorous than the other mothers, yet he had wanted her to be just a little less theatrical, to laugh more quietly.

Most of all, he hoped that she would allow him to be the important one—just for once. The time he had won the state's most important swimming medal, she somehow managed to take over the proceedings by announcing that he had obviously inherited his swimming talent from her. She had gone on to tell, at great length, how she had been an accomplished diver in her youth. Only days earlier, she had attempted to regale people at a dinner party with an elaborate tale of how she had always been terrified of the water.

Well, now she was in London, and he and his dad were here. Earlier, the thought of his dad's being in danger had made him feel sick to his stomach. At that moment, and for the first time, he had realized how important their friendship was. He couldn't remember feeling that kind of closeness with his mother—so why did it make him feel so guilty? Finally, no closer to understanding the way things were, he fell asleep.

■In the next room, Jim felt surprised. Surprised because he'd only been drinking coffee. Surprised, consequently, because he felt so calm. He was positive the idea of Jan Mulder being blown out of the water contributed enormously to his relaxed feeling.

For the moment, at least, there seemed to be no immediate threat to him or to Jake. Still, he wondered whether he'd feel so secure if the guards weren't on duty outside. But he knew the real source of his security was Max. He knew Max would never allow any harm to come to Jake or him. Max was the one person who'd believed in Jim all along. It was Max who came up with the theory that someone had drugged Jim before the shareholders' meeting. He alone believed that the terrible scene that followed had been deliberately planned to discredit Jim—to destroy the Carson Toy Company. Now it seemed the chief had been right all along. Jim tried to remember the shareholder who'd given him the glass of wine before he spoke that day. Everything remained a mystery. Then he tried to remember how Jan Mulder had looked. He drew another blank. Still, he'd only met him that one time, when he was thirteen. The only thing he could recall was an older man with a lively interest in computers. No matter how he tried, the face would not come to mind. Of course, if he *had* been drugged, and now he was certain of it, Mulder could easily have arranged for any number of people to do it. He looked at the clock—12:30 A.M. Better sleep. Cairns and an important business meeting tomorrow. So much for Sunday being a day off! He fell asleep wondering if rich men—like his father had once been—were simply born demanding. They probably just learned to shove people around more as they gained more power.

112

chapter ten

Max sat up in bed sipping his third hot chocolate. A near-empty packet of Scotch finger biscuits was on the bedside table, beside his latest *Police Gazette*. His wife, Jeannie, was sound asleep in the other twin bed. Over the years, she had trained herself to sleep through late-night telephone calls, late arrivals, and early departures. In the early years of their marriage, she'd worried every time he was a few minutes late. Now she simply left several cups of hot chocolate in a Thermos beside his bed and went to sleep. Max looked at her affectionately and dunked another Scotch finger in his mug of chocolate. The last call had merely confirmed his expectations—Jan Mulder had already disappeared without a trace.

He made a couple of entries in his notepad. Things he wanted to follow up in the morning. 1. Jake's grandmother, Joyce: (a) what's she remember about Mulder? (b) got any pictures? 2. Interpol: shipping schedules/drugs. 3. Who bought Mulder's company when he left Oz after the lawsuit. 4.

Check *Herald* newspaper, *Fin. Review.* Any info on Mulder. He closed his notebook. The one note the chief didn't need to make dealt with the most important point of the investigation for him. Max reckoned Jan Mulder couldn't possibly run an operation this vast on his own—not with all the computers in the world. He merely used the school's mainframe to communicate both locally and abroad. So who were the people he contacted? Interpol could handle the overseas problem, but what about the local situation? Who else in Australia was involved? Where were they now? And were they strangers or people he knew? For the moment, he decided to keep a few ideas close to his chest. When he'd meet the people from Interpol tomorrow. morning, he'd decide which way to play it. He checked his watch. Hell! it was Sunday already. He decided he'd better try to get a few hours' sleep before Martin picked him up. In less than two minutes, he'd finished his chocolate and cookies, turned off his bedside light, and begun to snore.

■Martin Oliver collected the chief at 6:30 A.M. precisely. As Max got into the sedan, he muttered, "Hope the oil I got on my jacket just now won't stain this upholstery, Martin." He burst out laughing when he saw Martin's stricken look. "Just kidding, old son. This car of yours'll be the death of you."

Martin was grumpy. The chief smiled and sipped coffee from an insulated cup designed to be used in a car. "And don't look so nervous—this thing doesn't spill."

"I wasn't even thinking about it," Martin said unconvincingly. "And how can you be so damned bright at this ungodly hour anyway?"

"Years of practice, Martin, years of it. Now, you know the routine?"

"Better go over it again. I'm not trained for cloak and dagger. Schoolboys stealing library books is the closest I ever got to crime until now."

"How 'bout concealing evidence? *Just* kidding. My God, you're serious at this hour. Anyhow. We have a meeting with the young American cop organized. You better get to know him a bit before you introduce him to Jake. You clear on your story?"

"He's supposed to be the son of a friend—I'll say I met him with his father once, when we were on vacation."

"What about Anne?"

"We agreed it'd be easier if they had never met."

"Good. Well, if you'd met a teenager, he likely was more interested in getting away from you as fast as he could."

"I relate well to young people"—Martin couldn't resist a dig—"unlike the police."

"Ah, it's all the same. They call cops pigs and academics eggheads."

Martin winced. "I suppose they wouldn't invite either of us to a party."

"Too right! I think it's best if you don't overdo it and appear too palsy-walsy. After all, you're supposed to be his new principal. I think all you have to do is agree on where and when you met, what you talked about in L.A., that kind of thing."

"Maybe we should discuss one of our programs he was interested in, or—"

"Martin, you'll blow it if you don't keep it simple. Remember, he's supposed to be jet-lagged. Nobody expects him to get into great detail. Anyway, young Jake is just about the brightest kid I ever met."

"No argument there."

"If anyone could find out a fake, he could. So let this boy tell his own story and do his job."

"I hope he's all right. Seems awfully young to be in this line of work."

"He's got quite a story. Tony Orsini. Eighteen but looks fifteen, maybe sixteen. Helped the LAPD smash the biggest crack ring they ever had. Selling through schools too."

"His computer accomplishments on his résumé were impressive."

"You'd be a better judge of that kind of thing than me. Ah, there's Lee. You can park right beside the squad car."

"Well, I just hope this Tony is as good as his publicity." Martin switched off the ignition.

"I hope so too. Because for the next few days we're married to him—for better or worse—as they say."

"I gather the *they* in this case means the CIA?" Martin asked.

"Partly. But it's mainly Interpol," Max said, undoing his seat belt. As he opened the passenger door he greeted Lee. "Good morning. You look a bit tired, son."

"Morning, Chief. Mr. Oliver. And if I look wasted, I'm not surprised." He smiled. "Betcha I feel even worse than I look. Big party last night."

"You'll live, son, you'll live. Now let's go and see what this young Tony Orsini's like. I hope to God he's in better shape than you are this morning."

■Just a few miles away, Jim's cab pulled up outside the Sydney domestic air terminal building. As he paid his fare and waited for his receipt, a uniformed chauffeur approached him. "Mr. Carson?"

"Yeah?"

"Mr. Jim Carson of Carruthers and Waterford?"

"That's right."

The chauffeur closed the door and the taxi drove off. "I'm the Sydney driver attached to Nufenix Corporation—and I know you were booked to fly to Cairns this morning."

"Still am, as far as I know."

"Slight change of plan, sir. Our directors have requested we take you in the private jet—it's going back up to Cairns, and you won't have to change at Brisbane."

"This is unexpected, but—"

"They called Mr. Carruthers with the change, but he said he imagined you'd already left for the airport. There's a phone in the car if you'd like to contact him?"

"No, I guess it's okay. But where do I get the plane?"

"I'll drive you to the airport at Bankstown. Car's just over here," he said, leading the way.

Jim followed. "I better cancel my flight."

"We took the liberty of doing it for you, sir." The chauffeur opened the door.

Jim stretched out in the back of the limo. He tried to remember the last time he'd experienced the luxury of a limousine and private jet in one day. A long time ago, he realized, just before the family company had gone to the wall.

■They were on their second pot of coffee when Tony Orsini announced, "I gotta tell ya man, criminals don't scare me half as much as schoolteachers and mainstream cops do."

Max, Martin, and Lee were taken aback by the good-natured American boy.

"Teachers I can understand, but other cops?" Lee asked.

"Well, I nearly got blown away by squad car cowboys on a drug bust in Washington, and the same thing happened in Miami. Guess that has something to do with the way I feel. Anyway, we tend to work a bit unconventional sometimes. I don't know about you guys, but American cops play everything by the book."

Max smiled. "I'm afraid we do too. Most of the time. Trouble is, if we get creative and something goes wrong, there are at least thirty other authorities that can crucify us."

"I understand how it happens all right," Tony said. "But sometimes people walk away scot-free while the paperwork clogs up the action."

"I suppose there's nothing you can do about it," Martin said.

"I do plenty when I have to." The other men heard the steel in Tony's voice and were just beginning to feel uncomfortable when he turned on the charm again. He looked like the brother everyone would love to have had. "Heck, guys, you can't exactly be going by the book yourselves. You've covered too much turf for that."

"We felt a few shortcuts were appropriate in this case," Max said. "We've had a few favors from people we can trust."

"I don't trust anyone," Tony said simply. "Not where drugs are involved. So much money. So much power involved. People screw up."

"Yes. Well, uh"—Max was uncomfortable—"we hope the danger is past in our neck of the woods at least."

"But you're still afraid of the revenge thing, right?"

"I don't want to be, but yes, I am. This Mulder seems too slick."

"He's that all right. Our shrinks figure he's compulsive. If he planned on doing something to Jake or his father, he won't give up. He may see it as a personal failure if he does."

"He's a drug addict too," Lee said.

Tony said, "I'm not being rude, man, but do you think I'd be here if I didn't know that?" The statement was delivered in a way that wasn't offensive. But it said, *I know what I'm doing, let's not waste time.* "His experiments were based on the work of Wilder Penfield."

The principal perked up. "The Canadian neurosurgeon?"

"Right on."

"What has this got to do with the Carson family?" Max said irritably.

"Plenty. Mulder had an idea that he could invent a game where he could tap into the human brain. But it's easier to follow if I show you this." He held up a videotape. "It's a dub of an eight-millimeter film. It was taken in a drug rehabilitation workshop in Amsterdam. Mulder had gone back to Europe after his scrape with old Jeremy Carson. He turned to shit. Got into heavy drugs. Smack and worse. They had a workshop program where people talked their problems through. What I've got here is a film taken illegally. Without patient knowledge or consent. Someone I know traded drugs for this film. We just got it. Furthermore, we smuggled it into this country. And now that you know all that, you also know that if you watch it you're violating every privacy act in the free world." He gave them a boyish grin that was totally disarming. For a moment he looked about fifteen years old. "Well, you guys wanna see Tony's home movies?"

The principal and the young cop looked decidedly uncomfortable. Max thought a moment and said, "Damn right we do!" As Tony snapped the cassette into the portable playback unit, Max cautioned, "Of course, we may have trouble remembering we saw any of this. . . ."

Tony looked jubilant. "You guys are *my* kinda cops. Yes!"

Half an hour later, the chief, Lee, and the principal felt decidedly intimidated. When Tony played the videotape copy of the film, they realized that the only person in the room who understood Dutch and German was Tony. Max and Lee didn't mind having him translate the scratchy soundtrack for them half as much as Martin Oliver did. It was embarrassing to have someone under twenty—and especially an American—explain to him a language he had studied and obviously forgotten!

The content of the film had been very distressing. Each patient had spoken about his past, the way he felt, and his future plans. Mulder had been extremely frank, and obviously drugged when he spoke. He was uninhibited in his description of his hatred for the family who had stolen his ideas. He admitted to having been a neurosurgeon in the past, but survival instinct must have stopped him from explaining just where he had operated. He described the procedure whereby the brain could be exposed and various parts of it stimulated with electrodes delivering around three volts of current. "We touched some areas and the patient said he tasted almonds. Other areas triggered other sensations. Colors were seen. One woman recalled past experiences, terror and laughter could be triggered, it was easy. Just a matter of applying the electrode to the critical part of the brain." When the counselor asked Mulder how the information would influence his future, Jan's face had contorted with cruelty. "I will make money any way I can. I will spend that money on research. And I will destroy the Carson family completely. I will also take the game they stole from me and modernize it. It will be a game where there is no fantasy, everything that happens will be real. Absolutely real to the player. The player who loses will be killed. Will actually experience real death while playing my game. And yet that player will survive to play another day. The world will see where the superintelligence comes from once again!"

When the tape had ended, Tony played an audio recording. It was an interview with an eminent neurologist from Holland. The man explained the Mulder he knew today. "Clearly brilliant, but he is also a paranoid and totally drug-dependent personality. This is a dangerous—potentially deadly—combination. He claims to be ahead of his time—and again, he may be right, although I hope not. He calls virtual reality *virtual history*. He believes computers and something like ultrasound can be used to replace the electrodes that pinpoint parts of the brain. He also thinks—and I pray that he is wrong—he thinks this process will one day enable him to record emotions." The tape ended.

Lee broke the silence that followed. "What good would all of this recording emotions do?"

"I can give you a terrible example," said Tony. "Say he kills someone, maybe in a horrible way. He records everything they feel while they're dying.

Their fear, their pain, all their sensations. Then he digitally plays back this death recording through the brain of someone playing a game. Maybe a war game, say. That means whoever plays actually experiences the death of the original person."

"And the player doesn't actually die as well?" Martin asked.

"No. Theoretically anyway. For the first time, you can experience death without dying."

"I can think of a lot of other things you could experience—some quite nice," Lee said with a vicious twinkle in his eye.

"Me too." Tony grinned. Then he was serious again. "But if Mulder can actually do this, and we believe he can, imagine the power he'd hold over the entertainment media. Take the pressure-sensitive gloves and computer images they use in virtual reality—that stuff would become obsolete overnight."

"If he applies it to computer games like he says he will in that movie, we should all be extremely frightened." Martin shuddered. "The bloodthirsty ones all have death as the penalty for losing."

Tony added, "Death in all kinds of bizarre ways. Say he applies this principle to Doomkritters—he said he wanted to anyway. When these weird kritter things gobble up the players who goof, what happens?"

"The players die—on the screen, anyway," Lee said. "Sometimes you bleed to death, sometimes you drown, like when the crocodile gets you."

Max said, "I have a terrible feeling he's been having the odd dress rehearsal around here."

"Seems that way. He won't have any scruples about sacrificing people so that others can live vicariously—or worse, die vicariously."

The chief quietly turned to Martin and asked confidentially, "What's 'vicariously' mean? I don't want this kid to think I'm an ass."

"In this case it's like living an experience through another person."

"You have to wonder who he intends to kill for real—so someone else can experience death without dying."

"Precisely."

"Shit—we better stop this maniac, but fast."

"We gotta find him first," Tony said. "But what I want to follow through on is this big thing he has about the Doomkritters game. Unfortunately, I don't know a lot about it."

"Hardly surprising," Martin said. "It died out after Sega and Nintendo captured the market. The only people who play it now are into cult games."

Tony looked puzzled.

"You know, games like they played in the arcades in the seventies, like the original Space Invaders."

"But you'll soon know all you need to know about Doomkritters. No one in the world understands it better than young Jake Carson. He and his dad are the reigning experts around here."

"Seems weird to me they still play it, man."

"Because it represents the family's financial downfall?"

"Right. Especially since the grandfather got

snuffed in the same way players who lose the game die—how weird are these Carsons anyway?"

"Not weird at all. I think it's just a game they enjoyed playing from the time Jake was in first grade. Jake is mature for his age; had to take a lot of things in his stride. Other boys in his situation would have cracked up. But you'll soon see what I mean. You ready to go and meet him?"

"Let's do it!" Tony said. He grabbed his luggage and followed Martin Oliver to his Jag. Just as they'd placed the luggage in the trunk Lee came running up to them with a big grin on his face.

"Got a message for you, Tony—from your boss."

Tony noticed Lee's hands were empty. "Where is it?"

"Verbal. He said to tell you in person."

"Why are you laughing, man?"

"It's the message. I'm to tell you to remember two things. One, remember you're only supposed to be sixteen. Two, if you meet any local girls on this assignment, keep your 501s buttoned up."

Tony turned red. "That weenie loves to embarrass me." He made a futile attempt to explain his situation. "Last job, there was this girl—well, actually she was a beautiful young teacher and . . ." He saw Lee and Martin were amused. "Aw, forget it. Let's get outta here!"

chapter eleven

"We're on our final descent, sir." The steward took the seat across the aisle from Jim and fastened his seat belt. There had been no other passengers, no conversation during the entire flight. Yet every time Jim had wanted something, it had materialized as if someone had read his mind. The breakfast had been freshly cooked and beautifully presented. Everything was first-class, from the Spode china to the elaborate sterling silver service. Afterward, he had killed the time watching a movie. The aircraft had a superb video projection system and a library of at least twenty first-release films. As landing became imminent, the screen filled with a closed-circuit color picture of the Cairns runway. The Lear jet taxied to a stop and its steps hydraulically lowered. A limousine pulled alongside the aircraft as Jim stepped down. The chauffeur jumped out. "Mr. Carson, I'm Horst—your driver." His neatly tailored uniform had a Nufenix Corporation logo on the breast pocket. Casually Jim thought he must be hot in this tropical climate with his shoulder-length blond hair under the cap. Horst gestured to the stretch Mercedes. "I'll be driving you to your meeting." Jim got in the passenger cabin and the car sped away. As they left the main road and headed through the cane fields he was puzzled. According to their annual report, the Nufenix offices were in a new building in the Cairns Central Business District. He picked up the intercom handset. "Have your people relocated?" he asked Horst. "I understood your offices were in downtown Cairns."

"They are, sir, but because it's Sunday the venue for your meeting has been changed. We'll be there in about twenty minutes. If you'd care to watch some television, the controls are on your armrest." The small screen glowed and a menu appeared. Jim pressed 3 for CNN, a cassette started, and a recording only two hours old replayed news taped off the satellite.

The limousine turned into a rough track and threaded its way through the cane fields. Jim felt uneasy. Something was bothering him. He looked at the back of the driver's head. The coarse long blond hair seemed matted. The driver caught his look in the mirror. He picked up his intercom, and his voice came through the speaker. "Our leader was afraid you might become homesick, Mr. Carson. So we have some special footage for you to watch. It's very recent."

A new picture replaced the CNN news coverage. It was so unexpected that it took Jim several seconds to realize he was watching himself. And Jake. He was outside his house getting into the cab for the airport. Jake was waving goodbye. The video cut to what must have been an hour later. His mother, Joyce, was dropping off a package. There was Jake answering the door, the camera followed her back to her car as she drove off. Jim felt sick. He grabbed the intercom and yelled into it. "What the hell is going on here? Who *are* you?" The driver replied calmly, "You'll know soon enough, sir. You might as well relax: the doors are sealed—there's nothing you can do until you meet our leader."

By now the Mercedes had approached the storage shed. As it rounded the corner, an entire corrugated iron wall lowered itself into the ground and the car drove onto a concrete pad. The wall raised itself to rejoin the roof as the car descended in the darkened shaft. Jim felt panic. His grip on the handset tightened. He felt the sweat on his forehead as he yelled, "If you've done anything to harm my boy, you'll regret it more than you can begin to imagine." He hammered his fist against the thick plate-glass window separating him from the driver. "Now for Christsake, stop this crap and stop it now! You hear me, now stop it!"

The driver calmly turned and gave him the kind of look people give puppies who can't seem to learn the most basic of commands. "You can't stop anything now, Mr. Carson. Don't you see, it's simply too late." With that, he removed his cap. The blond hair was attached to it. Jim felt a wave of nausea as he realized the chauffeur was a skinhead, the stud in his left earlobe a tiny silver swastika.

■ "Okay, you win easily. Where'd you learn to hold your breath that long?"

"Dunno, Tony, from diving I guess. You're pretty good yourself."

The boys toweled themselves dry and caught their breath. They'd just completed their fifth contest to see who could stay under water longer.

"Great pool. This is where you teach diving, hunh?"

"Yeah. All our competition stuff's held here too. One of the best pools in the state."

"With some of the best talent I've seen." Tony nodded toward two girls sunning themselves on the pool surrounds. "Maybe we should try and pick them up?"

Jake felt awkward. "I don't know . . . I—"

"You like girls don't you?"

"Yeah, sure. They're okay."

"You mean you're fifteen and you don't have a steady?"

"Not yet. Anyway, I just turned fifteen. But I'm taking Carol Anne to the swimming club dance next month, though."

Tony realized he was forgetting the age difference. Just three years older than Jake, he'd only gotten semiserious about the opposite sex after his sixteenth birthday. He decided to cool it. "Ah, well. What should we do now?"

"I got the keys to the computer lab—Egghead Oliver gave them to me so I could show you. Guess I shouldn't call him that in front of you."

"No problem. He's a friend of my dad's. I don't

know him except for meeting him with my parents." He kept glancing at the girls as he spoke. When they caught him looking, they giggled. "Well, I guess we should get changed and go?"

As they headed for the locker room, one of the girls said, "Gonna introduce us to your friend, Jake?"

He stopped dead in his tracks. "How come you know my name?" he asked, surprised.

"We watch you practice your dives sometimes."

"Yeah," said her friend. "We gave you our wet Speedos award."

They both burst out laughing. Tony smiled and Jake felt like an idiot.

"Thanks, I guess. Well, this is Tony. He's from L.A."

"I'm Karen, this is Kylie."

"Hi. So don't I get a wet Speedos award?"

Karen teased, "You aren't wearing Speedos."

"Nope. This is my patriot swimsuit. Note the stripes on the front, stars on the back."

As the boys walked away, Kylie called, "I notice they got the stars in the right place!"

"Whatya mean?"

"She just gave you the best buns award!" The girls dissolved into hysterical laughter.

"Deal with you ladies later," Tony said as they went inside the locker room.

"I like these Aussie girls, yes!" he said to Jake as they headed for the showers.

"Those two are pretty friendly all right." Jake thought they looked like a lot more fun than Carol

Anne. Maybe they were a bit old for him, but still, if they gave him their wet Speedos award he couldn't look *that* young.

Tony finished his shower and was pulling on his 501s by the time Jake joined him at the lockers. "Be right back, Jake old buddy, just want to ask those ladies a question or two." He sprinted out to the pool area as Jake began drying his hair. Suddenly something on the tiled floor caught Jake's eye. It was a wallet, and someone had obviously dropped it. He opened it to find a wad of American and Australian notes inside. There was also a current California driver's license bearing Tony's picture. Jake was surprised he had a license. But maybe California let you have one at fifteen. He read the date of birth. Quick calculation made him realize that Tony must be just over eighteen years old.

"Oh, you found it," the voice said over his shoulder. "Musta dropped it."

"Sorry, I didn't know whose it was and—how come you got a license, man?"

"Uh. It's a long story. Fake ID. Gets you into places where you need to be sometimes. I mean, it just helps if you're dying of thirst and want to buy a beer." He held his arms apart, palms upward. "Hey, old buddy, it's no big deal."

Americans, thought Jake. "What about the girls?"

"Gone. They'll be around again I imagine. After all, it's gonna be a long hot summer, right?"

"Guess so." Jake thought this summer could be a lot of fun if he had a friend like Tony Orsini around. Tony was one cool dude.

■ "Our leader will see you now, Mr. Carson." The skinhead who called himself Werner had already shown Jim to his room. "And please don't try to get away again. You'll only wind up with another bruise on your head."

"Who the *hell* are you people?"

"You'll be given a full explanation in a moment or two. Now come with me."

Werner applied his thumb to the laserscan pad, and the door glided open. He gestured Jim to walk ahead of him down a narrow marble hallway. Jim considered trying to take the gun from Werner's holster and shoot his way out—until he saw the video surveillance cameras lining the corridor. Too much organization. A door at the end slid open, and Werner escorted Jim through, into one of the most beautifully furnished apartments Jim had ever seen. Original oil paintings by the masters lined the black marble walls. Priceless sculptures and antique furniture crushed the rich burgundy broadloom, and Strauss crystal chandeliers graced the elaborate thirteen-foot ceilings. Werner pointed to a comfortable morocco leather chair in front of a massive marble table. "Sit here. Our leader will join you shortly." He stationed himself in a nearby alcove. A perfect position for surveillance. More and more, escape seemed an impossible fantasy. Jim heard a motor whir, and a mirror in an elaborate gold-leafed frame glided open to allow a man in military uniform to enter. As he came in, Werner clicked his heels and saluted. The man ignored him. He walked to the table and took a chair opposite Jim.

"I trust you find your accommodations satisfactory?"

Jim forced himself to speak evenly. "Look, whoever you are. I came for a meeting with Nufenix, and all this—this craziness is really over the top."

The man silenced him with a gesture.

"It must be very confusing for you, Jim. We have met, you and I. Of course I looked a bit different the first time we spoke." He clicked his fingers and Werner brought a file that mysteriously seemed to appear from nowhere. "This is closer to how I looked, although these pictures were taken about thirteen years before you were born—thirteen years before we met, in fact. Look at them."

Jim opened the folder. There were three people: his father Jeremy, his mother Joyce, and a man he recognized. But who? The three were standing in front of an old aircraft.

"Oh God, no." Jim wearily closed the folder and looked into the man's face. "You're Jan Mulder."

"With some extensive plastic surgery. But you missed out on another photograph. The second time we met. I had this face all right, but I wore a beard and glasses. Let me show you a picture—"

"It's not necessary." Jim's voice was flat. "I know your eyes. They've been in my nightmares for years now. You're the man who gave me that glass of wine to drink before the last shareholders' meeting."

"Very good. The Carsons are so incredibly clever."

"Look, I don't know what you think my father did to you or why this vendetta—"

Mulder interrupted. "It was a mixture of LSD and a concentrated extract from peyote—you were very dramatic, you know."

"What the hell do you think—"

"Shut up!" Jan was in a sudden rage. His face blackened as he spat out his words. "I am in charge here. This time I have an invention that will change entertainment forever. My last major invention was stolen by your family. Then they made out like I was crazy. You know how it feels when they think you're crazy, don't you. My organization dropped me. Said if I was too incompetent to patent an invention they couldn't trust me to run the operation here. Trust! I trusted your father. That was my mistake."

He had calmed down a bit. Jim was cautious. "But how can this affect us? We were ruined financially. I lost my business, my wife left. If my father did everything you say he did, and if—"

"If?" Jan was screaming again. "You dare to say *if*? Your father forced me to go back on drugs. At a time when I couldn't afford them. If it weren't for him, my whole life would have been different. We all could have been friends." Suddenly he was quiet and looked very tired. "Werner . . ."

"I know, sir, I know." Werner moved calmly and spoke reassuringly. He touched a button under a painting, and it swung open to reveal a small refrigerator. He removed a silver tray and presented it to Jan. "Perhaps I should do this for you?" Jan nodded and offered his arm.

Jim watched in fascination as Werner applied the

tourniquet, then injected the contents of a hypodermic into Jan's vein. He removed the tourniquet, swabbed the needle mark, and applied a tiny Band-Aid. He returned to his position in the alcove. Slowly, Jan brightened. "So you see, when you can afford the drugs, there is no drug problem. Perhaps you'd care for something? A drink perhaps? No need to look so apprehensive, you won't be drugged. Werner, bring a sealed bottle of anything Mr. Carson wants from our bar."

The skinhead opened an antique cupboard and placed a fresh bottle of Johnnie Walker Red on the table with an ice bucket and a glass. "Your brand. Never opened," he said smugly.

Jim did not ask how they knew his preference. He decided to waive his no-drinks-till-six rule, opened the bottle, and poured a couple of ounces on three ice cubes. He took a long sip. "Mr. Mulder, I don't want to annoy you, but are questions allowed in this interview?"

Jan's gesture was an invitation for Jim to proceed.

"You seem to be doing okay. Whatever my father did hasn't exactly ruined your life."

"Not my business, perhaps. But at a time when I was building a new social life, he destroyed my chances. I would have liked a normal home, recognition of my abilities, my accomplishments. I was earning a place in the community. Your father made sure that could never happen. However, I survived. He didn't. I used my knowledge of the drug underground to build my own empire. And after I proved myself to the party, they accepted me again. Now they realize how my invention can raise even more money for our cause."

"This, uh, *cause?*"

"The same as it always was. To rise once more. To prove we are subservient to no one. And, first of all, to cleanse this world of those who are unworthy. We know certain undesirable characteristics are inherited. Characteristics that weaken the world, and, naturally, there are those who should be snuffed out. We moved too slowly last time. But take your specific case. Your father placed financial greed ahead of science. That made him unsuitable as a human. Obviously he has passed on his contaminated genetics to you and your son. And so there's only one option—break the chain forever. It's regrettable but—" He made a gesture that said, "What can one do?"

The enormity of his words sank in.

"But you can't kill us . . . you'd never get away with it. I mean, people know I was coming here today, my company, the plane, the cars, the—"

"You are much simpler than your father. Much nicer, too, I imagine. The plan is this. We will do our business, you will invite your son up for a day here. He will play his part in finalizing my invention, then we will all fly back to Sydney. It's very simple."

"You don't intend to destroy us?"

"Of course not. The Nufenix jet will simply have an accident. It will just happen to explode over the Coral Sea. Four people will perish—you, your son, the pilot, and me."

"You would sacrifice your own life—just for revenge? You must be mad!"

"It's you who must be mad. It will only *appear* to be me. I have already organized a whole new identity. A few people will mourn the Carsons perhaps, but the world will rejoice to hear a Nazi war criminal is finally dead."

"But this company—it's respected—it's one of our top one hundred. And this invention you spoke of."

"My shares were transferred to an international conglomerate on Friday. So everything is perfectly clean. There's no connection with this company and politics. The worst that can happen is not too ominous. Oh yes, people may learn that a former major shareholder was undesirable, that's all. The others on our board, as well you know, are pillars of the Australian community. Nobody will be more genuinely shocked than Sir Edgar, our chairman. But I have great faith in the establishment. Little will be printed. Little will be said. Much of the money from the invention will ultimately fund our cause. And since your son has temporarily disrupted our drug business, we may experience a shortfall for a few months. But like my favorite inspiration, the phoenix, the business and I will rise again. Now to practical matters. You are to telephone your son and tell him to come to Cairns. I need him to play a rather special game of Doomkritters."

"That is one thing I will never do. No matter what you do to me. Jake has nothing to do with any of this."

Mulder laughed tonelessly. "Nothing? He broke a code that's jeopardized a business, that's costing us millions of dollars a day. You call that nothing?"

"But Jake's just a boy. All he did was find a computer disk you left in the wrong place. Why should he pay for one of your mistakes?"

Mulder slammed his hand down on the table. A guttural howl seemed to start way down in his throat. Werner ran to the table, and Jim shrank back. Saliva dribbled from the corner of Jan's mouth as the howl turned into a screaming shout. "Your son is just like his grandfather—he'll do anything he can to discredit me. Because of him our leaders are asking questions again. Wondering if I've become careless . . . questioning my personal habits. And it's your son who's responsible. Well, he is not going to get away with it, he . . . shall . . . not!" With that, Jan Mulder abruptly became still and he stopped yelling. His entire body sagged, and he buried his head in his hands. "Werner," he whispered, "make him go away now. You see what they're like? I told you . . ."

"Do you want me to deal with things while you rest awhile?"

Jan stroked Werner's hand. It was a gesture filled with gratitude and love. Werner looked at Jim with contempt. "Look what you have done to him now."

Jim was bewildered. "I only asked him—"

"Get back to your quarters. You've already upset him enough for one day."

"*He's* upset! What about me?"

"Your problems are of no interest to me." Werner looked down at his hand. Jan was still stroking it. "I intend to see that the culmination of his work takes place tomorrow as planned. And above all, I intend to see that your family does no further harm to him." Then he turned to Jan. "It's all right. I'll fix an injection. You'll soon feel much better—everything is going to be just fine, Father."

chapter twelve

"Man, this is so *retro*," Tony said as they finished another game of Doomkritters.

"Yeah, but you still haven't cracked the code," Jake said.

"Like how?"

"Like, f'r instance in the old PacMan, you're between two ghosts, right? You see if one of them is looking away?"

"Yeah, I know that one. You could go right through the ghost who wasn't looking in your direction."

"Right. Well, in Doomkritters, there's a trick with the crocodile."

"What is it?"

"See if you can figure it out."

"Aww, c'mon, man, give a jet-lagged American a break."

Jake laughed. "Only because you're a tourist. Well, you can usually avoid the crocodile by moving left. He's only programmed to turn right once you're under the water."

"I get it. Like the old arcade games. Always had a system you could use to beat 'em."

"You want another game?"

"Think I better split. The principal's wife is supposed to be making us dinner. Next question is how do I get there?"

"I'll walk with you. It's just around the corner. Just let me grab my bike so I can ride back."

"Okay. Hey, where's your old man? Thought you said he'd be home by now."

Jake locked the front door behind them. "On a business trip to Cairns."

Tony looked intense. "Where?"

"Cairns. It's in far North Queensland. Why, is something wrong?"

"No, not at all. Let's get over to Egghead Oliver's place. Shit. Now you got me calling him that."

"Better be careful." Jake laughed as they hit the road. "Oh no, talk about bad luck!"

"What's up, man?"

"Lila Spooner and her dog. Heading our way."

"She's the one you told me about?"

"Yeah."

"I thought witches had cats, not dachshunds."

They both tried to control their laughter as Lila and Heidi approached. Lila focused her beady eyes on Jake. "And just what do you think you're laughing at?"

They exploded into a fresh outburst.

141

She looked increasingly annoyed. Then she stared at Tony, and her tiny eyes widened in alarm. Nervously, she pointed a bony finger at him. "I know who you are. You don't fool me one iota!" And she hurried off. Jake thought she looked frightened.

"Weird," was all Tony said. But Jake thought his new friend looked lost in thought. And worried.

■Jim was back in his room. It must have been the most luxurious prison ever conceived. Although he hadn't been hungry, a superb lunch had arrived late in the afternoon. He had decided to force himself to eat—if only to keep up his strength. But once he started eating, he had actually enjoyed everything. His mouth twisted ironically as he thought about condemned men and final dinners. He wondered what they had in mind for him now. Werner said he'd visit later to arrange for Jake's arrival. Well, let them try anything—he wouldn't betray his boy in any way. While he was home, Max was nearby. Sooner or later someone would smell a rat and then . . .

A motor hummed, and his door slid open. Werner entered. "I understand you enjoyed your lunch. The chef is an accomplished *cordon bleu*, you know."

"If you're here to try and make me pull my son into your trap—"

"That will all be later. We understand he is well guarded at the moment, so of course it would be very bad timing. He is expecting you home in time for dinner, however. I suggest you send him a message saying you've been delayed. A nice thought would be to have a pizza delivered. I notice on your credit card statements this is a typical treat?"

"I'm not doing a thing to help you maniacs. When I don't show up on time he'll call Max and—"

"Your chief of police."

"You got it. And then the questions will start."

"Very well, have it your way." Werner consulted his electronic memopad. "We'll have a fax sent from the local Hilton to your favorite pizza delivery service and they can do the rest. Your son will receive a meal with a message from his father apologizing for the delay. We have your credit cards. You can even pay for it. Or rather, your estate will." He smiled at his sick joke.

Jim thought quickly. "All right. I'll do it. If he's going to receive a message, it might as well be from a member of the human race."

Werner's hand moved so quickly Jim never even saw it coming. All he felt was incredible pain as the skinhead's fist connected with his sternum. "That is level-one pain. It can go as high as five, if you care to continue your insults." Jim was doubled over and gasping for breath for several minutes. Finally he said, "What the hell do you want me to do?"

"Telephone them. Tell them to deliver the boy a dinner. With a message you've been held up till tomorrow morning."

"That's it?"

Werner entered a code to activate the telephone. He passed Jim the handset. "Do it."

■ Jake arrived home to hear the telephone ringing. By the time he got the door open it had stopped. The light on the answering machine was blinking. He pushed the replay control. As Joyce's unmistakable voice swamped the room, Jake turned the volume down. "Jake, it's your grandmother. You must be out I guess. I just wondered who you were with today. Lila dropped by with that sausage creature of hers and I was a bit worried. So give me a call." A series of tones followed, then, "It's me again. Just wondered if you were home yet."

Jake figured he'd better return her call. Once his grandmother got on the message machine she was relentless with her calls until someone returned them. Oh well. He pushed autodial.

"Grandma, it's Jake."

"You sound like you're chewing gum again."

"Yeah."

"You know what it does to your teeth."

"It's sugarless," he lied.

"I hope so. You got my messages?"

"Yeah. And I was with Tony. A new kid. Mrs. Spooner figured she knew him."

"She says he's definitely the one she saw running away from the school when they had a fire and—"

"Grandma, he just got here this morning. The principal's a friend of his dad's. He brought him right here from the airport."

"Oh, that's strange. She's convinced she also saw

him running from your house when I was cleaning yesterday."

"It's not possible, Grandma, like I said, he just got here this morning."

"Well, you know how she is. Still it never hurts to check, does it. Is Jim back yet?"

"No, he was supposed to be but—maybe the plane was delayed."

"That's probably right. Time to spare, go by air, I always say."

As Jake was wishing she'd get a new line concerning air travel, the doorbell rang.

"Gotta shoot, it's the door."

"I heard. Talk to you later."

"Bye, Grandma." He hung up. The doorbell rang again. "I'm coming," he yelled in the direction of the door.

"Oh hi, Ritchie. I didn't order anything."

"It's your lucky day, dude. Your old man phoned from Cairns. Said he won't make the last flight to Sydney, so he'll be back tomorrow."

"Why didn't he phone here?"

"Beats me. Maybe he was just making sure you ate. Anyhow, he sounded real busy. Just gave the order and said to charge it and to tell you he'll see you tomorrow."

"Okay. Maybe he tried to phone when Grandma was leaving one of her messages."

"Dunno. Hey, I thought you guys hated anchovies. You always dump on me when Kerry forgets and puts 'em on."

"Yeah, that's right."

"Well, your old man said to make sure you got triple anchovies."

"Yeah? You must have heard wrong."

"Nope. Anyway, this is a weird night. This other guy came in, just after your old man phoned this through. He pays for three four-seasons, family size, to be delivered to an address that he writes down. I go there just before coming here, right? They don't know anything about it. I said well, they're paid for and this is the address the dude wrote down, so must be a surprise."

"What'd they say?"

"The guy says it's not a surprise, it's an insult. Take it back. Turns out they're vegetarians. Then I come back to my van so I can come here, and there's some dude running away from it. Maybe he was planning on stealing a pizza? Totally weird night."

"Totally."

"Well, enjoy. See you at school tomorrow."

"Thanks, Ritchie."

Jake shut the door. His dad must be losing it or something. *Triple* anchovies! *Oh well, just pick off more of 'em than usual.*

■ "I tell you there's something wrong. All these signs have pointed to control in the Cairns area, Jake's old man goes to Cairns, he doesn't show on his scheduled flight, and you say this is normal? Shouldn't the alarm bells be ringing by now?"

Max Pink sighed. "I know it looks bad, Tony, but Nufenix is one of the country's most respected companies. Lee has tracked things as far as Banks-town airport, it looks like they took him on the company jet. We're trying to track the cab that took him to the airport."

"Does Jake know anything?"

"We're attempting not to alarm him. Don't forget, this is probably just a coincidence."

"So who did his father go to see?"

Max consulted his notes. "A director. Name of Peters. Mr. I. T. Peters. So far, we've been unable to reach him."

"What about the boy?" Martin asked. "Is he safe?"

"The Commonwealth people are there until midnight, and then I take over," Tony said. "Anyway, I'm planning on going earlier. Have a few ideas I want to follow up."

"Maybe you'd care to fill us in on them this time?" Max was irritable now.

Tony gave them his best innocent smile. It made him look fifteen. "Ah, heck, you old guys just wouldn't understand!"

Max fumed. "What I don't understand is why Lila Spooner saw you. She's been blabbing about you all over the place. She placed you at the school fire and you didn't even let us know you were near the place. If you'd told us, we could have coordinated and—"

"Hold it right there, Chief." Tony was serious now. "When I got here, all we knew was there was a huge drug operation with a control around this area. Back home, you never know who's involved.

And there's been so much publicity about corruption in high places in Australia. Just a minute ago you said the Nufenix director must be okay because he has a title. Well, some of your jailbirds had titles too. I know you guys are okay now, but what if there'd been a bad apple in your department? Anyhow, do you tell the Commonwealth cops everything you know?"

Max looked embarrassed. "I guess I deserved that. But the point remains that the advice we've had from international people hasn't always been sound."

There was an awkward moment.

Martin said, "We kept quiet before to humor international authorities. We all have regrets about that. And if we're a bit hypersensitive, it's just that we're personally very fond of Jim Carson and his son."

"What about the grandfather?"

"Hate to say it," said Max, "but when he died the only person that really cared was his wife Joyce. He was a ruthless character, obsessed with money."

"Look where it got him, hunh? Wow, look at the time. I better get over and start my surveillance outside Jake's. In the meantime, think about getting us to Cairns. If things move the way I think they will . . ."

"I suppose I can tell our international connection a little secret." Max half-smiled. "There's a jet at our disposal, fueled and ready to go. And a helicopter plus a helluva lot of backup is in place up north."

Tony looked at Max with admiration. "You really must fool a lot of people with this folksy routine, Chief."

Max laughed out loud. "You speak for yourself, you—wide-eyed innocent!"

The tension between the two policemen was over for the moment, but each kept a few secrets he was not about to share as Tony left the house.

■Jake turned on the television, grabbed a Pepsi, and opened the pizza. There was an envelope fastened to the inside top of the box. He felt his head start hammering as he saw the lettering on the envelope.

E2C1F2G1

He was familiar enough with the code to know it spelled his name. His hand was shaking as he removed the envelope from the lid. It was a single piece of paper. It read:

D1B3G2G2G1A3D2B2D1C3C1F3F1

He grabbed a pencil, and a minute later he'd translated. The message simply said BULLETIN BOARD.

He raced to his room and switched on the computer. When he and his friends wanted confidential communication, they communicated on bulletin board. If you had a modem, you left a message on bulletin board. Each subscriber had a number. But to read the message, you had to enter your number, then your PIN. Jake entered his number. The screen read:

WELCOME TO BULLETIN BOARD JAKE CARSON
NUMBER OF MESSAGES WAITING: 2
PLEASE ENTER PIN

Jake entered his personal code. It appeared on the screen as ****.

The first message had been left yesterday.

Hi Jake, don't forget the swimming carnival dance Saturday week. We're having a party here first so come around seven. Stay cool. Joanna.

P.S. Did you hear about Drew? Wrecked his mother's Mercedes when they were on vacation. Wasn't supposed to drive her car, now he's grounded for months. Ha! Ha! Serves that little poser right!

P.P.S. Don't eat before you come Sat. Dad's barbecuing hamburgers.

SAVE MESSAGE?
NO · NEXT ·

As the screen filled with the code Jake's heart sank. He reached for the disk labeled CODEBREAKER.

chapter thirteen

In the yellow car parked down the street, Tony heard Jake whisper, "Oh no. Not Dad. Please . . . no."

Tony ripped off the headphones and sprinted toward the house. As he neared the gate, one of the Commonwealth boys materialized. "Oh, it's Wonderboy," he said.

"Yeah, sure," Tony said impatiently. "Anybody come to the house?"

"Why's that?"

"You know damned well I don't have to give a reason."

The guard sighed. "Only the guy delivering pizza."

"There was no call out. Would've picked it up."

"Oh yeah?" He was suddenly interested. "Well, the pizza guy left just before you got here. They talked at the door. Obviously friends from school. Said they'd see each other tomorrow. You sure you got nothing on the wiretap?"

"A couple of calls from his grandmother to the answering machine, then one back to her. Then something on a modem just as I got here, but it hasn't been analyzed yet. Anyway, I'm going in. Stay on it."

The guard was hostile again. "Don't need *you* to tell us that. We're here another half an hour. Anyhow, it's a waste of time."

"Sure hope you're right."

■Jake looked dejected as he answered the door. Tony could see by his eyes he'd been crying. "Hey old buddy, what's up? Can I come in?"

"I'm kind of busy. Homework and stuff. You know."

"Just for a minute?"

"Okay. Just for a minute then."

"You got anything to drink?"

"Yeah, if you like."

Jake wished Tony hadn't shown up. The message in the code had really dealt him a body blow. On the other hand, he was glad Tony was there. He needed a friend in the worst way right now.

"Jake. Where are you, man?"

"Just thinking."

"Hey, pizza—where'd you get it? Looks a bit cold."

"M-my dad sent it." Jake bit his lower lip to stop it from trembling.

Tony pretended not to notice. "All the way from Cairns? No wonder it's cold."

—"He called the pizza place here and told them to deliver it. Said he was held up."

"Hey, we could reheat it?"

Jake turned away, trying to keep it together. Tony walked to him and put his hand on his shoulder. He felt Jake stiffen, then relax. "Hey old buddy, seems like you need a friend. What's happening, man?"

"Nothing I can't handle."

"Well, if you're sure . . . Look, I'm staying at Egghead Oliver's so if you want anything call me, okay?"

"Yeah. Sure. You okay to let yourself out?"

"Yeah. I'm okay."

The minute the door closed, Jake returned to his computer. He reread his translation of the message:

> Your father sent you this dinner. We have him here in Cairns. If you mention any of this to any person—any person at all—you will never see your father alive again. If you want to save his life, behave normally. Be inside the international terminal by the Qantas ticket desk at 8:00 A.M. tomorrow. Follow these instructions to the letter or else. Expect no further communication. Our people are watching you. Who can you trust these days? Not even yours truly, Old Redders.

Defeated, Jake didn't even bother to follow usual shutdown procedure. He simply reached behind the Power Mac to shut it off. Something cold touched his finger. Curious, he rolled out the computer stand. A wireless microphone dangled behind the monitor. It had been positioned with double-sided tape, but it had slipped just enough to be felt when he had reached for the power switch. Someone was bugging his room—*again!* He looked out the window. The guards were stepping into their car. They drove away. He felt vulnerable. Yet the message clearly expected him to behave normally, so there must be no immediate danger. As the Commonwealth car drove away, it slowed as it passed a yellow car parked in the street. The brake lights on the parked car flashed briefly. Was it a signal? Or had a driver momentarily touched the brake pedal by accident? Then Jake remembered. He'd seen the same yellow car the night he'd been knocked out. Suddenly he had to know if the people bugging his room this time were connected with that car. If they were, he could get the license plate number. Maybe he could use it to help his father in some way. Just how, he wasn't sure, but it was the only lead he had. Then he could decide whether to go to Max . . .

■In the yellow car, Tony heard Jake talking to himself. "Oh well, might as well watch TV for a while." He heard the TV set come on and turned down the volume on his receiver. *Jeez, Jake, are you deaf?* he wondered. In his rearview mirror he saw the lights of a car approaching slowly. As it got nearer, he saw it was an old VW convertible. A tire had just gone flat, and the car rumbled to a stop just ahead of him. The driver got the car to the curb, killed the lights, and got out. It was a young woman. Tony saw she had a body to die for. She looked at the tire, then looked around helplessly.

Tony made sure his transceiver was still on record and got out to offer assistance.

She smiled. "What a bummer—flat tire."

"Never mind, if you got a tire jack—"

"You sound like a Yank!" As she spoke Tony noticed her eyes flick to his left, and he knew he'd been had. Before he could move, something stung the back of his neck and everything turned into slow motion. He felt his leg muscles going limp. He watched her pour a bottle of bourbon over his face and place the bottle by his hand. Then everything went black.

■Jake turned on the front porch lights and walked onto the verandah. He held an envelope in his hand and assumed the appearance of someone going out to mail a letter. As he neared the yellow car, he slowed down. The door was ajar but there was nobody in it. He continued walking and surreptitiously noted its license number on the envelope. He continued walking to the mailbox. He mimed posting a letter and quickly stuffed the envelope in his pocket. He walked slowly back home, but the street was totally deserted. This time he stopped by the car. In the still of the night, he heard the distinctive soundtrack of the video he had started earlier. His hunch had been right. Whoever owned this car was watching him. He looked inside, and his eyes started to sting. On the floor in the back he saw the towel and the stars and stripes swimming shorts Tony had worn at the pool. He ran to the house chanting under his breath and keeping time with his footsteps: "Tony traitor, Tony traitor, Tony traitor."

Back at the computer, Jake had finally regained some of his cool. He desperately tried to convince himself he'd been wrong about Tony—probably lots of other guys had patriot swimsuits as well. But there was that business with the driver's license. And Lila Spooner. Convinced she'd seen Tony before he said he even arrived—before the chief and Egghead Oliver said he'd arrived. They couldn't all be lying, could they? Or was this thing so big that they were all part of a terrible drug ring? Was Tony part of an American Mafia link? Jake had to know. He powered up and loaded AeroRez. A few minutes with a contraband disk altered the standard airline program. Five minutes later, he'd hacked into the airline computer system. Passenger lists were supposed to be confidential, but if you knew enough . . .

Today's passenger list showed no Orsini. He started working backward through previous flights. When the name finally appeared on the screen, the information made him feel empty and incredibly sad. Lila Spooner had been right after all. Tony Orsini had arrived a week earlier than he said he had. That meant there was no one to trust here. Not the chief, not the principal, not the young cop Lee, and most disappointing of all, he could never trust Tony

Orsini again. Thank God for his dad. Oh, please let him be all right. He had to do exactly what they said. There was no other way. He felt dizzy as the message from the code went through his mind over and over again: "Our people are watching you. Who can you trust these days?"

chapter fourteen

The radio operator at Street Rescue was having a slow night. By this time, they'd usually collected half a dozen intoxicated street people. But tonight the hostel was almost empty. So when the anonymous call came through that a dark young man was lying drunk in Walker Road, the volunteers arrived in record time. "C'mon, pal, let's get you in the back of the van. Can you walk a bit?"

"I . . . I gotta get. Police. The . . . ch . . . Max, he'll tell you. Ohhh."

"Now just take it easy. Wow, wouldn't want to light a match near you. That's it, one foot in front of the other. Nearly there now."

The two-way radio crackled in the Street Rescue van. "You got a client on Walker Road?"

"Bringing him in now. Can't tell you who to notify, though. He's got no ID."

"Anything else?"

"There are two unlocked cars here—a VW with a flat and a yellow Datsun. He could have been with either vehicle—or maybe neither of 'em. You want license numbers or—"

"Fax them to the cops when you get here—with his description. Maybe *they* can figure out who he is."

■Lee was rounding the corner of Walker Road to check out Tony when they announced the plate numbers on a stolen VW. As he approached Tony's car, two things hit him at the same time. Tony was nowhere to be seen, and the plates on the VW in front of it were the same as the numbers they'd just announced. He leaped out and checked the cars: both were empty. There were jumper wires hanging below the VW dash. He ran back to the car and radioed base. Twenty minutes later Max and the police physician were attempting to get some sense out of Tony. "His blood's clean. Point oh-oh-oh-oh alcohol. But look at his pupils. He's got something else in there. And that needle mark in the back of his neck. We could biopsy a bit of the skin there, Chief."

"No, there's no time for any of that stuff. Look, Doc, what have you got to snap him out of this?"

"I *could* try a mix of antihistamines and Stymacardyne, but it might give him one hell of a headache later."

"Do it."

"It's a bit irregular unless—"

"So is everything else about this case."

"You're the boss, Chief."

"Spread it around."

■An hour later Lee saw the chief's car pull up. He ran over to the passenger side as Tony rolled down the window. "Phew! You stink like—"

"Don't say it—you oughta smell it from here! Anyway, what's going down now?"

"Jake's still in his room—closed his curtains about twenty minutes ago. Maybe you should try and talk to him?"

"It's pretty late for someone new to be dropping in." He looked at Max. "What about you?"

"I don't know what to do. If we follow our instructions, we just maintain surveillance until someone makes a move. If I follow my instincts, I think these geniuses we've been listening to are all wet."

Max's car phone rang. "Max Pink . . . you have . . . good . . . uh-huh . . . yeah, I see. What else . . . he did? How the hell did he do that? . . . I see, yeah, thanks a lot."

"What's up?" Lee wondered.

"They've analyzed the wiretaps—Jake's been using his modem a bit—calling bulletin board."

Tony asked, "What's that?"

"Local computer club info bank," Lee said. "Kids use it to communicate with each other."

"Trouble is," Max said, "they have their own passwords, so it could take forever to figure out what he got in or out of it. But we got one thing definite—and you're not going to like this, Tony. He hacked into the airline passenger list file. He's been checking on arrival dates."

"You figure he knows I got here earlier than we said?"

"Count on it."

Lee sighed. "There goes our credibility."

"Whew! This is bad. He'll never trust us again. What do we do now?"

Max seemed deep in thought.

"Chief?"

"I hear you. It's just that I'm making a decision I wish I didn't have to. Because it will likely land me in shit right up to my badge. But I think we simply have to tell Jake the whole story—tell him everything that's going on."

"Man, am I glad you said that. Let's go in."

From the darkness of the living room, Jake watched the three cops approach the house. He'd already decided the best plan was to do exactly what the code message said. Maybe if he followed the instructions to the letter, his dad would be okay. Yet he still hoped against hope that the guys approaching the house had nothing to do with his father's disappearance. But this was no time to take chances. The best thing was to avoid any communication with anyone until tomorrow. He raced to the kitchen and threw the back door wide open. He grabbed the handle that pulled the concealed retractable ladder down from the attic ceiling. He ran up the steps and pulled the mechanism back up. From the main hallway, there was no sign of access to the attic. Now, with a little luck, they'd assume he'd left in a hurry.

When Tony finally picked the front door lock, the first thing they noticed was that the back door was wide open. "Looks like we're too late," Lee said.

"We'd better not be—look around, maybe the boy's scared—and who could blame him." He called out several times, "Jake, you there? It's Chief Pink, we just want to talk to you. Nothing to be afraid of, son."

No answer. They checked the house once more, looked in every cupboard, behind every door, before searching the back garden. As they walked back through the house, Tony heard a brief creaking noise from the ceiling. He gestured to the others to be quiet, then led them into Jake's room. The computer was on, the WP program banner active. As Tony typed, Lee and the chief watched his silent message appear:

TALK NORMALLY. THINK HE'S IN ATTIC. GOT AN IDEA.

As the two cops faked a noisy search, Tony swiftly loaded one file after another. Finally he found what he was looking for. "Bingo," he said under his breath. He couldn't risk the noise of the printer and copied off the screen by hand. Then he returned the computer to its original state and called the others. "We're just wasting our time here. Let's face it— he's gone."

His face was flushed with excitement as he showed Max and Lee the ominous message. They were grim-faced as its full implications sank in. Max spoke loudly, "Nothing more to do here. Lee, lock that back door, we'll meet at the police station to sort things out."

Leaving the house, they closed the doors and front gate as loudly as possible. Before Tony and Max got in the chief's car he whispered, "Lee—start your engine, then ring my car phone." He added loudly, "Tony and I will see you downtown."

Once both engines had started Max answered Lee's call immediately. He instructed him to drive away as noisily as he could. "Then circle the block and park nearby. I want you to keep this house under surveillance. Let me know when you're in position. Then we'll make sure he hears us drive away too. There's one helluva lot to do before anyone sleeps tonight."

■Jake heard the cars drive away and lowered the staircase. Cautiously, he descended. He left the lights exactly as they had been when the chief, Lee, and Tony had arrived. He had been lucky this time, but if they returned . . .

He loaded HotelRez and entered some information, gave them Jim's credit card number and confidential PIN. The system accepted the booking and noted that it was a firm reservation. If the guest didn't show, the charge was not refundable. Under special comments he entered:

GUEST IS CARDHOLDER'S NEPHEW. WILL MEET RELATIVES AT INTERNATIONAL TERMINAL 8:00 A.M. MONDAY. PLEASE ARRANGE TRANSPORT TO

The answer came back: CONFIRMED.

He cleared the screen and gathered what money he had, packed a few things in a small carry-on bag, and went out a side window that couldn't be seen from the street or the rear lane. He stayed in the shadows until he could climb the fence into the neighbors' yard. When he finally entered the lane he was four houses away from home. If he could get away without being seen for the next few minutes, he'd be okay. Luck was his. The bus pulled up as he reached the stop. Forty-five minutes later he was finally eating a decent meal and looking down on Sydney Harbor from his room in the Renaissance.

chapter fifteen

Jake arrived at the international terminal exactly when they'd told him to. To get to the Qantas area he had to make his way through a large group of Japanese tourists. He was totally unaware of the way it happened. He heard a voice from behind tell him, "There's a ticket to Cairns in your bag. Use it." There was no way of knowing who in the crowd had spoken. In an uncrowded area he saw they had unzipped his bag and placed the ticket inside. It was for an 8:45 flight—on a domestic airline. Jake ran outside and frantically hailed a cab. "I have to get to the domestic terminal in a hurry!"

"Not a problem." He made his flight with nine minutes to spare.

In the international terminal, the European cops were furious. Not only had they lost track of Jake, they'd lost face in a big way. Much earlier—around two A.M.—Tony and Max had told them staking out the Sydney airports was a waste of time. Max had said, "Jake's determined to go to Cairns—he thinks it's the only way to save his father."

"That's it," Tony said. "This maniac Redlum obviously wants him there in one piece, so he's bound to get there safely. That's why I am going to Cairns with the Commonwealth boys on the military jet."

"You're welcome to come with us," Max told them. "But once you get there, you're on your own. We've got us an old Bell chopper lined up, but all seven seats are booked."

■ Jim jumped as the door panel leading to his room glided open. It was Mulder, looking rested and full of anticipation. "Well, Jim. I trust you enjoyed a good night's sleep."

"Does it look like it?"

"No need to be churlish—I've come to show you something absolutely amazing. Something only an old Doomkritters player could fully appreciate."

"Oh jeez, what next?" Jim muttered as he followed Mulder into the hallway.

"We'll go up a level, so you can truly comprehend it."

They walked up a long metal stairway and paused before a silver door. "Prepare yourself to be astounded." He placed his thumb on the laser panel, and the door opened.

It was one of the most awesome sights Jim had ever seen. Mulder had taken the Doomkritters video game and built it for real. It was the magic of theater, of brilliant stage sets, and the effect was overwhelming. There were the mountains where the evil barbed-wire gorillas lurked. There was the quick-sand sea, golden and shimmering below. And every aspect of the game had been created life-size. The lighting was magic as it constantly bathed the creation in rainbows of fluorescing color. Mists and fogs swirled over the artificial landscape in breathtaking patterns.

Mulder was smiling broadly as he took in Jim's astonished reaction.

"But wait till you see the final triumph—the pièce de résistance. Behold, the crocodile."

He clicked a remote button, and a monstrous silver crocodile reared up from beneath a blue lagoon. Menacingly it snapped its massive metallic jaws as light flashed off its sharp stainless steel teeth.

"He's programmed to take the player in his jaws if the player makes the wrong move. And then he takes him under the water and holds him until— but you already know the game."

"You're really enjoying this, aren't you, Mulder? What a shame you didn't dedicate your talents to theme parks."

"Amateurs! They don't allow you to truly participate. This is different. Just imagine if you really were to experience drowning. And yet you could live to play the game again. This is the ultimate terror, don't you think?"

"What is the point of all this?"

"Follow me. Up here, the computer banks. As someone walks through the game, plays it, actually lives it, we record every electrical impulse his brain sends out. Later, in a living room, nice and safe, someone else plays the game. They'll wear a head-band capable of receiving the recording made here today. All the thrills, none of the danger. The good players will get through it. Losers—as in the real game—will experience what someone experienced here. An actual drowning. An actual death. Imagine the sensation! People will deliberately lose just so they can experience dying."

"Sick. Precisely how many do you intend to kill to make your horrible brain recordings?"

"For the moment, just two. You, and your son Jake."

■Fifty miles away Jake walked outside the passenger terminal at Cairns International Airport. As he looked around, two seemingly unrelated incidents occurred.

Horst guided the stretch Mercedes with the black windows into a no-standing zone outside the terminal building. A noisy troop of Boy Scouts had commandeered the area. Surrounded by camping gear and duffel bags, they seemed to ignore their leader's attempt to keep order.

A woman of Latin American appearance with a baby on one arm and a bulging suitcase in the other approached one of the Scouts near the limousine. *"Habla español?"* she asked, then in broken English, "You boys speaking Spanish, please?" As the Scouts turned to look at her, the suitcase she carried burst open. She cried out in Spanish as clothes, a hair dryer, and some carefully wrapped presents spilled out onto the pavement around the back of the limousine.

"Don't just stand there, boys, help the lady!" the scoutmaster commanded.

A flurry of activity concealed the woman's swift actions from everyone. She placed a small plastic object on the Mercedes's undercarriage. She heard a satisfying click as a powerful magnet secured the box to the car's metal. By the time the driver leaped out, the Scouts had picked up her things and were helping her repack. The driver looked around and shook his head in annoyance at the commotion.

He spotted Jake and gestured toward the car's rear door. He held it open for the boy to enter. Moments later, they had left the airport to journey northward on the coastal highway.

■ "Good job, Anita," Tony said. "We can pinpoint the Mercedes within a thousand square yards." He was following the radio beacon tracking signal on a small screen.

"Don't mention it!" she yelled over the chopper's whine. She no longer looked like the distressed mother at the airport. "I didn't realize how heavy babies are. You want me to monitor his car phone?"

"You're the electronics genius."

"It might take a few seconds to track them, but once they start talking we should get most of what they say. If they use it at all," she said.

Tony shrugged his shoulders and turned to talk to Max. They were deliberately flying high. The chopper had the markings of a local broadcasting station. Because it was regularly used in surf watch patrols, they hoped its presence wouldn't alarm Jake's driver. Max pointed downward. The car was turning into a cane field.

■ "Hey, where are we going, man?"

"To visit Daddy," the chauffeur sneered. He hated punks like this. Figured they knew everything. All this kid could do was look worried and chew gum. He'd better not put any in the clean ashtrays. The leader was very fussy about things like that.

"How do I know you're taking me to see my dad? How do I know you're telling the truth?"

The chauffeur really admired the leader at moments like this. He'd said this would happen. He picked up the mobile phone. "If you want, you can say hello. After that, just shut up. Otherwise you're liable to be hit on the back of the head. Okay?" He pushed an autodial preselect. "Hello, yeah it's Horst. The brat doesn't think he's going to visit his daddy. What do I do? Okay." He handed Jake the mobile phone. "He's gonna let him talk to you, but first up it's the boss."

Jake listened in fascination to the voice he knew as Old Redders. "Jan Mulder here—Old Redders to you, of course. I've told your father he can say hello. If he wants to say anything further, don't be surprised if you hear him screaming in pain. Here he is."

"Jake . . . son?"

"Dad, are you okay?"

"Yeah, I'm fine, son. I have a nice room, the food's good and—" Suddenly he screamed, "It's a trap! Get out! Get to Max—you can trust hi— aowwww . . ." Jake heard his dad's cry of pain, then a scuffle at the other end. He kept the phone pressed to his ear so Horst couldn't hear the commotion. Suddenly Mulder was back on the line howling at the top of his voice. "You put Horst back on the line! Now, you hear, NOW." Jake decided instantly. Listen to his dad. He pretended to continue talking as he opened the rechargeable battery cover with his thumb. He slid the cell out and shoved the metallic side of a chewing gum wrapper into the compartment. He pushed the battery back up and clicked its cover into place. There was a quiet hiss as the telephone's fuse shorted out. All the while, Jake had continued his fake conversation. "Okay, Dad—Dad, I can't hear you too well. This thing keeps cutting in and out. Dad?" He shook the phone and pretended to listen. "You there? Yeah, it's bad at this end too. Okay, talk to you there." Jake gave the phone back to Horst. "Cheap car phone you got, man—cuts in and out."

"They'll call back," Horst said, replacing it in its charging cradle. As he did, there was an imperceptible hiss as the charger shorted out. Horst failed to notice the standby LED on the handset had gone out—permanently.

◼ In the bunker Mulder was still screaming into the speakerphone. Werner came over to him and spoke smoothly. "Father, be calm, Father. There's so much at stake. We've obviously lost contact. You must rest for a moment."

"But something has gone wrong. You must go and find out!" He spun around to face Jim, who was hunched over in a chair. "By God you'll pay for this!"

Jim wiped the blood from the corner of his eye. There was a two-inch gash where Werner had hit him and cut him with his heavy swastika ring.

"You've already promised me the death penalty. What more can you do."

Saliva ran from the corner of Mulder's mouth. "If your son escapes, you'll die a horrible death."

"If he gets away from you maniacs, it'll be worth it—owww!" Werner slammed his fist into the side of his neck.

"Werner, deal with this pig later. You must go and get the boy. Immediately. If he gets loose in the cane fields and we lose him . . ."

"Horst won't let him escape. Anyway, they're burning off those cane fields tonight—if he hides, he burns, so—"

Mulder roared, "You dare to defy your father?"

Werner looked frightened. "Very well, Father, I'll go. But first, I think it would be a good idea if I got you a little something—something relaxing. You must be well rested for the final round."

The idea seemed to calm Mulder. "Yes, yes I must, thank you," he said as he rolled up his sleeve.

chapter sixteen

Jake was trying to figure it out. There were two things to do. Get out of this car and get away. Then get to Max. He figured they must be a few miles from the main road. They were driving slowly down a track beside a cane railway line. If he could get out and over the tracks, maybe he could make a run for it and hide in the tall cane fields. Then try to get back to the main highway. His heart was pounding.

"Hey, man, can you stop for a sec? I gotta take a piss in a hurry."

Horst looked dubious. "You'll just have to wait. My instructions are to take you to our leader—without stopping anywhere."

"Okay, it's your Mercedes. Don't blame me for wrecking the upholstery."

Horst was annoyed. "Can't it wait?"

"No, I can't. I had a lot of orange juice and coffee on the plane and"—he bent over in the back-seat—"I can't hang on any longer. Sorry, man."

"Don't! Wait!" Horst snapped as he braked. Mulder would kill him if he messed up his car. Besides, the kid wanted to see his father—he wouldn't try anything funny now. He released the electric door lock. Jake leaped out and walked over to the tracks, his back to Horst. He pretended to unbutton his 501s.

"Hey. Don't go so far away. Stay where I can keep an eye on you."

"You want to watch me do this? What are you, some kind of pervert?"

"Shut up and do it!" Horst looked straight ahead. He saw a flash of movement in his side mirror as Jake made a run for it. By the time Horst jumped out of the car, Jake was over the railway line and running for the cane fields. Horst considered grabbing the pistol from the glove compartment, then decided he'd lose too much time. He sprinted after the boy. When he got to the edge of the cane field, he'd lost sight of him. As he started to go into the field, a snake slithered out of his way. He recoiled in terror, ran back to the car, and snatched the mobile phone from its cradle. It was dead. He hurled it to the ground in frustration and opened the glove compartment to get his gun.

■ "There he is! Now give me the bullhorn and get in as close as you can," Tony said. The helicopter pilot buzzed the top of the cane field where they'd last seen Jake. They zigzagged the area and Tony talked into the bullhorn: "Jake, it's Tony. Look, man I know you think I double-crossed you. But what you're thinking isn't true. Show yourself and let us help you. There's no time to waste. Jake, come out so we can get you away from here. Please!" For a moment, they saw him. He was running from the helicopter. But Tony knew Jake was really running from the sound of his voice. He felt bad about that—real bad. Max yelled in Tony's ear, "He won't get far, let's get the car!" Tony gave him the thumbs-up sign, and the helicopter swooped toward the railway line.

■ Hearing the bullhorn, Horst panicked. His only thought was to return to base as quickly as possible. When he realized the helicopter had come back for him he was unable to make a decision—he always contacted the others for instructions. The helicopter blades whipped up dust in front of the car. He braked then reversed. The helicopter hovered patiently. He grabbed his pistol and fired at the undercarriage as he ran from the car. A machine gun spattered bullets on the ground in front of him.

Max's voice came through the bullhorn. "Drop it!" Horst decided he had to obey. "Now get back to your car, and spread-eagle over the hood— we're coming down for a visit." He ran to the car and flung himself on the hood. Max covered Tony as he came down a rope ladder thrown from the hovering chopper. Anita followed. They waved okay, and the chopper swung away to search for Jake.

"Cover me while I frisk him, Anita," Tony said. "Okay, he's clean."

Horst sized up Tony first, then Anita. "You're the lady with the kid."

"Surprise, surprise," Anita said.

"I like your Nazi earring!" Tony said. "Well, he's not going to be a Nazi for long if he doesn't cooperate."

"I got rights, don't forget," Horst snarled.

"Sure. And if my friends in the chopper were here, I'd probably have to respect them. But it's just you, me, and my friend here. We figure *we* have the *right* to know everything about this operation in record time."

Horst decided Tony looked too green to be a threat.

"I'm not saying a thing without a lawyer present."

"Seeing as how there are lives at stake, time is of the essence. I'm going right to the top," Tony told Anita. "With one of those new Mafia persuaders we, uh, confiscated in the Jersey crack bust."

"This I don't want to watch." She turned away.

"Okay, weenie, drop your trousers." Horst hesitated. Tony aimed and fired. The bullet raised a small cloud of dust and creased the heel of Horst's leather boot. "I said drop your trousers—*now!*"

"What the—" He did as he was told.

"Now I have a little present for you. Go on, take it."

He gave Horst a round plastic ring with a small key in the top. "Turn the key." The ring snapped open. It was hinged in the middle.

"Now take out the key and give it to me."

Horst was totally bewildered. He gave Tony the key.

"Now put it on."

"What? Where?"

Tony was casual. "It goes around the little bag that holds the family jewels."

"You're out of your mind, I won't—" The sound of the safety catch being removed made Horst decide to follow Tony's instructions. As he put the ring in place, it locked. "How do I get this thing off if—"

"I'll tell you when the time comes. Now pull up your trousers, you look ridiculous. Okay Anita, you can turn around now. Tell the boy with the busy barber about his new jewelry."

"Okay. You're wearing a very special ring, Horst—in a very delicate area. It won't hurt you, unless you try to remove it yourself or someone presses a remote control, like this one." She held up a small unit, about half the size of an audio-cassette.

Horst was looking decidedly nervous. "So what's it supposed to do? Give me a shock?"

"I'll show you with this one," she said, and tossed an identical ring several yards down the road.

She pushed the remote. The ring exploded, leaving a crater the size of a baseball in the road. Horst grabbed his crotch in reflex action. His face had turned ashen.

"Now," Tony said, holding the other remote, "are you gonna tell us everything you know about this operation, or do I push the button and blow your balls off?"

chapter seventeen

Jake figured he was far enough from the helicopter to get back onto the road for a breather. The cane fields were alive. He'd already dodged a couple of snakes, walked into a web belonging to a spider with enormous fuzzy legs, and squished several cane toads underfoot. Now he knew why they burned off the fields before harvesting the cane. As he came into a clearing he saw an old machinery shed about forty yards ahead. He walked toward it and saw a lone motorcyclist heading his way. He was about to run into the field again, but saw the rider. The guy was fairly young, just a biker. Jake waved his arms, signaling him to stop. "Hey man, I'm trying to get up to the main highway, can you give me a lift?"

"Not a problem. I can take you right into Cairns if you want. But you'll need a helmet."

"Oh."

"Cops are strict about it around here. Tell you what, I got a spare back at the shed. Want to go back and get it?"

Jake couldn't believe his luck. "Fantastic!"

"Hop on the back."

They got to the shed and went around the side. Jake noticed one wall was missing. As they rode Jake said, "By the way, my name's Jake."

The driver smiled. "I'm Werner." The wall began to rise as the concrete apron started its descent. "My father's been expecting you, Jake. Actually, so has yours."

■From her position by the car, Anita maintained radio contact with the helicopter. She constantly relayed Horst's information about Mulder's operation. Suddenly she heard Max's voice alter. It was filled with tension as he described what he saw through his high-power binoculars. "That must be the entrance to his operation," Max said.

Tony said to Horst, "Who owns the BMW motorbike?"

Horst was a study in cooperation. "Werner—his son. I told you about him."

From the helicopter Max said, "From what you tell me it's not well guarded, but it still sounds like a fortress. How do we get in, I wonder."

"Easy. We go in there in style. In the limo. So get your swat team down on the ground by the Mercedes. We've just renamed the Nazi driver the Trojan Horst."

■"Well, now." Mulder was calm for the moment. "We must proceed—finally. Had you gotten away, you would have destroyed our plans. Werner, bring the electronic headband for the boy."

Werner produced a high-tech aluminum briefcase and placed it on the marble table. Respectfully, he opened it. Inside was a metal ribbon padded in vinyl. A small antenna protruded from the back.

"I think this should be the right size—it can be adjusted of course. Put it on his head."

Jake looked at his dad.

"Don't worry, all it does is pick up signals from your brain and transmit them to the receivers placed around the sensudrome. Advanced microwave technology. Every impulse is recorded on twenty-four-track DAT. Later these signals can be edited—undesirable sensations removed, that sort of thing. The final recordings will be compressed and multiplexed into interactive playback modules. That will allow future players to experience in their homes what you are about to experience today."

"How can you store all the information in something small enough for a home game?"

"The same way I put all the workings of an original arcade game into a microscopic chip. The same way today's cheapest PC has the power of dozens of huge early computers. Just think of it—you will be stars. The first people to allow others inside your brains. Why, in the history of video games—"

"Father," Werner's voice held a warning note. "The time . . ."

"Yes, we must play the game. Shortly after dark we leave here with our tapes and"—for a moment he looked regretful—"all this disappears. I shall miss the paintings."

"You're going to trash this whole thing?" Jake asked, incredulous.

"No matter—our electronics are already being reproduced in Taiwan in a more miniature form. But come, I guarantee you shall be as impressed as your father was when he first saw my sensudrome. Werner, run a final check on the recording equipment. The game begins at seven P.M. precisely."

■ Outside the sun was setting and workers were lighting the evening cane fires. Max and Tony were explaining the map of Mulder's underground labyrinth to the group gathered by the limousine. With reluctance Horst had drawn the diagram in the dirt. He was sullenly surveying the group as Max reviewed the plan.

"Three of his people will be in this room operating the recording equipment." He addressed two of the swat team. "You guys can seal off that doorway as soon as we get in." They nodded. "Anita, you clear on your position?"

"Gary and I will be here, so we can control this hallway easily." She pointed out positions as she spoke. "That has to contain the other guards."

"That leaves Max and me," Tony said. "We'll go into the sensudrome itself using Horst as a cover. It'll be up to us to handle Mulder and his son. Where will they actually be, Horst?"

Horst couldn't keep his eyes off Tony's shirt pocket containing the remote control detonator.

"Horst, we need an answer and it better be right." Tony patted his shirt pocket threateningly.

"Okay, okay," Horst said, "the crocodile is here in the pool—it's the only part of the game they're recording with the kid. It's a huge tank at the end. It has a glass wall."

"Like an aquarium, you mean?" Max asked.

"It is an aquarium," Horst said. "Well, actually a swimming pool with one end made of plate glass. They intend to watch the underwater action from there."

"Jeez. What ghouls," Tony said.

"What's in the area by the glass wall?" Max asked.

"That's the nerve center. All the electronics, the generators and lighting banks. Plus they got chairs there so they can be comfortable."

"Lucky for them their pool doesn't leak," Max said dryly.

"Nazi engineers built it," Horst said arrogantly.

"Skip the commercial," Tony said. "Well, we're as ready as we'll ever be. Catch!" He threw Horst a mobile phone. "Time to dial the number, sweetheart. And, oh, Horst," he said, tapping his shirt pocket, "this phone call better be convincing." Horst swallowed hard. The chopper pilot looked concerned as he spoke to Max.

"I might have to move the chopper—the fires and this sudden wind—but I'll only be minutes away," the pilot said.

"We'll maintain radio contact." Anita checked her equipment.

Inside the Mercedes, Horst was talking to base. Through the heavily tinted screen he saw the cane fires suddenly shift direction against a darkening sky.

■ "And now, you get to play the final round. Now step onto the platform," Mulder commanded.

"And if I don't?" Jake said.

"Look above you. Your father is locked in that booth—the laser lock responds to only two thumb-prints—Werner's or mine. If it isn't opened within fifteen minutes, it will be flooded with cyanide gas. I think you will cooperate. Now get on the plat-form."

Jake stepped onto a metal platform suspended over the pool. It was a one-yard circle with a stand holding a joystick.

Mulder smiled in anticipation. "All you have to do is play Doomkritters as you usually do. The joy-stick moves the platform in any direction. You see the crocodile under the water. If you get past him, you win. But I warn you, he's like the one in the game. He can move just as fast. His sensors track you instantaneously. If he touches you, the platform tilts and he is programmed to take you and hold you under water. Just like the game. Now, once you're in your start position you can experiment with the controls. You have one minute to practice. If you're ready?"

A voice on the speaker system echoed through the sensudrome. "Sir, Horst is on his mobile out-side—requesting entry."

"That stupid ass! If I didn't need a pilot later—Werner, let the fool in." Mulder walked to the clear glass wall at the end of the pool and took a comfortable leather chair. Werner placed his thumb on the laserscan and entered the code that allowed the Mercedes and its driver access. Then he joined his father, taking a matching chair on his right. Champagne had been poured into the Lalique crystal flutes before them. They toasted each other, and through the pool's glass wall, they watched as the massive silver crocodile lay waiting under the water.

Suddenly the motors controlling the hydraulics whirred. Jake's platform moved out over the center of the pool. He experimented with the joystick. A display built into it read "SECONDS TO GAME START." The red numbers started their ominous countdown. 59 . . . 58 . . . 57 . . .

chapter eighteen

The Mercedes started its descent.

Tony was in the seat beside Horst. He fitted a silencer to his pistol. "You sure you've told us everything we need to know?"

"I told you I had." Horst was agitated. He was getting edgy. He needed a fix.

"I just can't imagine him having so few guards."

"We didn't think we needed them anymore—there used to be another six."

"Six more?" Anita asked from the backseat. "What happened to them?"

"He used them to record the first parts of the game."

"And?"

"They lost," Horst said matter-of-factly.

"And you figure it's safe to hang around this maniac?"

"He looks after me," Horst said simply. "Besides, he needs me to fly the plane out of here tonight. This is the entrance." He felt sick.

They faced a solid steel panel. As it glided into the ceiling a guard with a machine gun rushed over to the car. Excitedly, he shouted, "For God's sake, hurry up, the game's already star—" Tony powered down his electronic window and the guard instinctively started to raise his gun.

Thwuck! Thwuck! Tony's gun spat twice and the guard went down, a mixture of agony and absurd surprise on his face. The team leaped from the car. With incredible speed two of them bundled the injured skinhead into the trunk and slammed it shut. Tony ordered Horst to park in the doorway. As they ran to the main corridor to take their positions the steel door began to close down behind them. The sound of crushing steel echoed in the hallway as the door crumpled the Mercedes's roof, then came to rest a few feet above the floor. Horst walked to the sensudrome entry. Tony and Max shadowed him— crouching out of the security camera's range. Horst pushed a buzzer. Inside, Werner barely glanced at the door monitor—he was totally involved in watching the game. He recognized Horst, scowled, and pressed the remote control to open the door.

"So far so good," Tony whispered.

"Okay," Max snapped to Tony and Horst, "let's *go!*"

■ The sensors in the silver crocodile's eyes tracked him with electronic precision as Jake eased the joystick forward, then to the right. There was a blinding flash of metal as the creature's tail lashed the water and the huge metallic jaws opened. It reared up and snapped within a yard of the moving platform. Jake recoiled as a spray of water drenched his T-shirt and temporarily blinded him. He wiped his eyes and pulled the joystick back, then to the left. Again and again the crocodile's jaws snapped shut. It was getting closer, more accurate as its computer reacted to his position. He slammed the joystick hard right and forward. If he could just get through the opening. As the metal beast rose, Jake's heart pounded in terror. The sharp teeth glistened as it lunged toward him, its mouth wide open as its neck turned sideways in an attempt to engulf his head. He moved just in time to avoid being crushed in its cruel jaws. Not fast enough. The teeth sliced a piece of flesh from his shoulder. Blood ran from the open wound as his white T-shirt turned red from the left of his neck to his waist.

"Perfect! Perfect!" Mulder screamed, his whole body leaning forward in cruel anticipation of a kill. Jake's mind was running faster than it ever had. In the game, if you sped left and ahead at a time like this you could beat it. He took a chance. He slammed the joystick first left then hard ahead. The platform responded instantly. Mulder laughed hysterically. "I changed the rules! I changed the rules! Nobody outwits my game!" The crocodile followed Jake's every movement with lightning speed. He leaned hard left on the platform to avoid the attack. But the electronics were too fast for him. The pain in his shoulder made him cry out as his glistening killer moved in for one final furious onslaught. He was inches from death when his reflexes commanded his body to flee the danger. Instinctively he took a huge breath and dived into the shallow water. He attempted to swim away. The water magnified the size of the crocodile's closing jaws, and he knew he was powerless. The machined mouth closed firmly around his chest, imprisoning him. The crocodile was winning. He felt a rib crack as the beast held him firmly under water. He saw the water turning red around him and knew. As soon as his breath ran out he would drown.

Tony and Max stormed the area where Mulder and Werner were sitting. Mulder screamed to Horst. "Stop these people. Stop them *now!*" His eyes were wild, saliva dripping from his lower lip. Horst seemed unable to move. He was surrounded by fear. He looked at Mulder, then Werner, then Tony. His ability to make a decision was gone. He feared for his life; he needed a fix. He decided to run.

Now Mulder was frothing at the mouth and wailing. "You traitor! Traitor!" He pulled a gun and pointed it at Horst. Horst froze. Werner screamed, "Father! Not near the glass tank." Max ran to the edge of the pool and dived in. He was desperately trying to open the metallic jaws and free Jake. It was hopeless. He came up for more air and went down again. Horst decided his only chance was to stay near the tank—they wouldn't dare shoot bullets near the glass wall—if it were to break . . .

Tony raised his gun to Werner. Werner yelled, "Don't! Jake's father dies if you shoot me!" Tony hesitated for a moment. It was all Werner needed. In a blur of action he kicked the gun from Tony's hand and pulled a knife from his ankle sheath. He lunged for Tony and went to stab him in the chest. The knife hit the remote control in Tony's shirt pocket. The control saved Tony from death but activated the gelignite ring Horst was wearing. Horst screamed in agony as it blasted his body against the glass wall of the pool. The noise of the explosion and the sound of crumbling accompanied the roar of tons of turbulent water gushing into the room. Its unbridled force thrust jagged pieces of plate glass into the air as the wall continued to shatter. The blast knocked Tony over on his stomach. He attempted to wade to safety but Werner leaped on him, his knife raised high in the air. At that moment, a rush of water buried a huge shard of plate glass in Werner's jugular vein. In a gush of blood and water Werner was washed against the bank of electronic equipment behind him. The electronic gear had begun to spark and explode in a spectacular fireworks of total destruction. In the pool Max felt himself being pulled toward the jagged opening as the water rushed out. He hung on to the crocodile for his very life.

■As the water level subsided Jake started to breathe again. He had been certain of one thing only—death. Now, through his pain, he was dimly aware of Max and Tony helping him. There was a woman too. And the smell of antiseptic. And someone was talking about cutting hydraulic hoses. Then the pressure was finally off his chest. Now a newer smell

190

—familiar, like the brake fluid they put in his dad's car.

His dad! Don't let it be too late—he had to let them know!

"My dad. Hurry, he's in—"

"Take it easy," Max said. "He's safe in a room up there. We'll get him as soon as we get you out of this contraption completely."

"Listen. That room, it's cyanide gas. Hurry!"

"Jeez!" Tony was alert. "That's what the freak was talking about. Stay here, Max, I'm on to it."

Tony stopped for a moment by Werner's dead body, then sprinted from the room. He took the stairs three at a time. He opened the door and yelled, "Jim, get out now! There's cyanide gas set to go any minute!"

But Jim was already running to Jake. "How is he?"

"He's going to be okay. He'll need a few stitches, though. Helicopter's coming back soon's they can land safely—there's still a cane fire all around us. Don't worry, Anita's highly qualified, she's handling the first aid till they get here."

■The smell of the recent fires would hang in the air for days. Still, the survivors were grateful to be outside in spite of it.

"So everyone's accounted for—except Mulder." Max was thinking out loud.

"And every*thing's* accounted for except those tapes he was recording," Tony added.

"According to our pilot, when the wind changed this whole area was ablaze for an hour. He couldn't have gotten through a fire like that and lived."

"Where are all the prisoners?" Jake wanted to know.

"There aren't any. When we opened the door to get them, they'd been shot."

"Did Mulder do it?"

"Obviously."

"And the guard we locked in the trunk finished himself off with a cyanide capsule," Anita said with a shudder. They braced themselves against the blast of air as the chopper landed.

While they were waiting to board, Jim asked Tony, "One thing I'd like to know."

"Yeah?"

"I thought the laser locks only opened if they sensed two thumbprints—Mulder's or Werner's. So how did you open all the doors—especially the one leading to my personal gas chamber?"

"You really wanta know?"

Jim nodded.

"I borrowed Werner's thumb. Don't look so shocked." Tony smiled his boyish grin. "Werner doesn't need it anymore!"

■ "Ooh, this kitchen stinks." Jim grimaced as they walked into the house.

"It's the pizza with the triple anchovies," Jake said.

As they cleaned up the house Jake had left twenty-four hours earlier, the telephone rang.

"Tony, it's for you. Take it in the other room if you want, sounds official."

As Tony left the room, Jim asked, "How would you feel about having someone help us run this place—full-time?"

"Depends on what she's like. Now you know that thing at the company meeting wasn't your fault, maybe you can handle it without so much scotch?"

"Owww! You have a point. What if we go for dinner together—you can meet her and think about it?"

"It's your life, Dad, you've got to go for what makes it work for you."

"Let's talk some more later," he said as Tony came back in the room.

"Mystery solved," Tony announced. "Found a body in the cane field. Burned beyond recognition. He had some tapes in his arms. They ran a check on dental records and guess who?"

"Mulder," Jim and Jake said in chorus.

"Yes!" Tony said triumphantly. "We gotta celebrate this. I'm buying. Don't worry, I got it in my budget. My bosses want me to see how you'd feel about training for undercover, Jake old buddy."

"No kidding. But the old man would never let me."

"Is this true?" Tony asked Jim.

"As someone told me recently, 'You've got to go for what makes it work for you.'"

"There's one thing we have to do, Dad," Jake said, and left the room for a moment.

He returned with the Doomkritters cartridge unit and joysticks. He handed them to his dad.

"You're right," said Jim. He tossed the pieces into the trash bag to join the dead pizza with the triple anchovies.

epilogue

The plastic surgeon considered several moments. Finally he spoke.

"It will be long and painful, and I cannot guarantee total removal of the scarring from your extensive burns. However, I can make you look acceptable. But you must realize this is a tedious, exhausting procedure for me to undertake. My fee would have to be around thirty percent higher than what we previously agreed to."

The man's charred lips contorted into a smile of sorts. "That will be no problem."

"In that case, welcome to Argentina."

About the Author

Ted Ottley was born in Canada but lives in Sydney. He has been a teacher, a journalist, a scriptwriter, and a boatbuilder and has worked in advertising and owned a recording studio. Ted Ottley is also a composer who has written the musical score for *Huckleberry Finn* and other television series playing around the world. He is also the author of *Code of the Roadies*, the companion to *Code of Deception*.